Real As It Gets

RUMOR CENTRAL

RESHONDA TATE BILLINGSLEY

Dafina KTeen Books
KENSINGTON PUBLISHING CORP.
http://www.kensingtonbooks.com

DAFINA KTEEN BOOKS are published by

Kensington Publishing Corp.
119 West 40th Street
New York, NY 10018

All Kensington titles, imprints, and distributed lines are available at special quantity discounts for bulk purchases for sales promotion, premiums, fund-raising, and educational or institutional use.

Special book excerpts or customized printings can also be created to fit specific needs. For details, write or phone the office of the Kensington Special Sales Manager: Kensington Publishing Corp., 119 West 40th Street, New York, NY 10018. Attn. Special Sales Department. Phone: 1-800-221-2647.

KTeen logo Reg. U.S. Pat. & TM Off.
Sunburst logo Reg. U.S. Pat. & TM Off.

ISBN-13: 978-0-7582-8955-1
ISBN-10: 0-7582-8955-3
First Kensington Trade Paperback Printing: January 2014

eISBN-13: 978-0-7582-8956-8
eISBN-10: 0-7582-8956-1
First Kensington Electronic Edition: January 2014

10 9 8 7 6 5 4 3 2 1

Printed in the United States of America

For Mya and Morgan

. . . who are forever keepin' it real!

Author's Note

When I was a little girl, I loved reading and writing. I loved to read a story, then rewrite it. I never knew that something I enjoyed so much would turn into a lifelong passion. But I am beyond thrilled that I get to create these stories for readers like yourself.

A lot of people always ask me where I get my inspiration. I get it from people like you—yeah, you holding the book. I can see someone like you out at the coffee shop, in the grocery store, or sitting in a classroom, and my mind starts to churning. The creative part of me goes into overdrive as I start asking "what if?" and begin creating stories.

I am eternally grateful to find people who appreciate my creations. So I begin this note from the author with a huge thank you—to all of the readers who crave my stories, who discover and appreciate what I write, and who continue to spread the word. It is because of you that I am what I am.

I also must give major love to my own drama queens, Mya and Morgan, who both wanted to help me write this book. At first, as the proud mommy, I was going to let them write a chapter or two. Then, they presented me with a written contract, saying they wanted forty percent of my money! Of course, I decided to pass on that deal. (Leave it to my girls to try and make a business transaction out of everything.)

I also have to shout-out my son, my husband, and the rest of my wonderful family and friends who support and nurture my literary career. Much thanks also to my hard-working agent, Sara Camilli, my wonderful editor, Selena James, and the fantastic publicity team of Kensington Books!

Thank you to Yolanda Gore and Rhian Collier for helping me stay on task. You guys are the best assistants ever!

Thanks also to the thousands of young people who have read, and will read, my books. Those who have emailed, tweeted and sent constant messages looking for more teen reading, I hope you enjoy. Special shout-out to LANES (Loving, Assisting, Nurturing, Educating, and Supporting Teenage Girls) in Orlando, Florida; the young ladies of Alpha Kappa Alpha Sorority, Inc., EYL programs; my wonderful Jack and Jill members; and all the youth groups and book clubs across the country who have supported my work. Thanks also to my wonderful teachers who laid my literary foundation, especially Lillie Lacy and Dr. Jocelyn Reed.

Thank you to the parents, teachers, librarians, and concerned adults who are putting these books in young people's hands, as well as to all my friends on social media. And finally, thank you to my fabulous teen advisory board, which helps me keep it real.

Well, enough from me. Make sure you hit me up and let me know what you think. If you've missed the other books in the series, please make sure you check them out!

Much Love,
ReShonda

Chapter 1

The image on the screen gave me chills.

I knew Savannah Vanderpool. She was a beautiful former Miss Teen Miami who had branched out to movies. We'd taken some modeling classes together when I was in middle school and although I didn't talk to her much anymore, we kept in touch through Instagram and Twitter. It wasn't often that I gave other girls props. But Savannah had earned hers. She was Beyoncé, Ciara, and Meagan Good rolled up into one. A class act, that's who Savannah was.

Was.

Because this chick I was looking at right then, was anything but classy. She looked like a crackhead, meth head, and dope fiend rolled up into one.

Savannah's eyes were sunken, almost like her face was swallowing them. She had dark circles around her eyes and her face was taut and dry. Her skin was sagging, looking like it was just hanging on to her bones. Her once-beautiful blond hair was stringy and the dark roots were showing. The only modeling she could do now would be in a "just say no" drug ad.

"Maya," my director, Manny, whispered in my earpiece. "Go! You're live!"

I caught myself. I didn't usually let anything get me off my game when I was in hosting mode at my talk show, *Rumor Central,* but seeing Savannah's picture had definitely left me speechless.

"Wow, I guess you can say I'm a little stunned myself," I continued, turning my attention back to the camera. "If you knew Savannah Vanderpool like I knew Savannah Vanderpool, you'd be just as shocked."

We'd gotten the story about Savannah being arrested just minutes before I was going on the air. My producer, Dexter, had handed me a sheet with some limited information and told me to wing it. I had no problem with that because dishing dirt was what had made me so popular on *Rumor Central.* I was even used to dishing dirt about my friends, especially because I was usually the one who had dug up the dirt. Even though I'd stopped airing my friends' dirty laundry, I had no problem digging in other celebrities' backyards. I had to. Since I started *Rumor Central* four months before, it had become one of the hottest gossip shows in the country. We were now shown in seventeen major cities and my popularity was through the roof. Celebs as big as Usher and Rihanna called me when they wanted to "slip" out a little gossip, and other celebrities tried to become my best friends to keep their dirt off the air. So, a little scandalous story never shocked me. But this picture of Savannah—I wasn't ready for that.

"This is just in to the *Rumor Central* studios," I continued, "so we haven't been able to get all the details, but rumor has it that this mug shot is from Savannah's arrest last night after she caused a scene at the *Sports Illustrated* reception. Apparently, she arrived to the event high, dazed, and acting out. Witnesses say she was actually in a psychotic-like state. Organizers saw her and refused to let her go on stage. We're told Savannah was so high that she took off all her clothes and began running through the party screaming and crying as she destroyed everything in sight."

I took a deep breath as an earlier photo of Savannah as Miss Teen Miami flashed on the screen.

I continued. "Our sources tell us Savannah was high on K2, a hyped-up version of Kush, the popular synthetic drug sweeping the country. We don't know much about K2, but you'd better believe that *Rumor Central* is all over this story and we'll keep you updated. I'm your girl, Maya Morgan, and we'll be back right after this."

I tossed to the break and motioned for my new assistant, Yolanda, to get me some water. Usually, we kept it light and gossipy on *Rumor Central*. I didn't get all deep into stories, and this was exactly the reason why. These kinds of stories were just too much.

"You okay?" Yolanda asked as she handed me a cooled bottle of Fiji Water.

I took a sip of the water. "Yeah, just trippin' over that picture." I glanced over at the photo, which was still up on the monitor. I'd seen Savannah about six months before and she had looked fine. How could someone get like that in just a few months?

Dexter came over to me on the set as Yolanda scurried away.

"Great job, Maya. I got some more details. Apparently, this K2 is more powerful than Kush, and it's getting really hot among celebrities. It looks like spices, or potpourri, and they say it was created in China or Korea as a plant growth stimulant. It's about ten times more potent than meth."

"Just wow," I said, shaking my head again at the picture. I knew some celebs that dabbled in drugs, but judging from the way she looked, Savannah had done a lot more than dabble. "I just can't believe that she's fallen off like that."

"Do you know Savannah?" Dexter anxiously asked as he ran his hands through his head full of bright red hair, something he did whenever he was excited. "I mean, personally? I figured you did since you know everybody."

Dexter was right about that. Before I was on-air—first as one of the five members of the *Miami Divas* reality show, then as the host of my own show—I was already at the top of the food chain as the leader of Miami's "It Clique," as one magazine had put it. In fact, that was why I'd been approached to do the reality show in the first place. *Miami Divas* hadn't done as well as they'd wanted, so they'd canceled it, fired the other four Divas, and given me my own show. That had been the smartest thing since the invention of the Internet, because in no time, I became the go-to chick for all the latest celebrity gossip, dirt, and entertainment news. *Rumor Central* had exceeded everyone's expectations and had even been picked up by networks in several other cities.

My BFF, Sheridan, had been one of the original *Miami Divas* who was fired, and that had led to a whole lotta drama, but we'd squashed that and were back to kickin' it. I couldn't say the same about the other busters from *Miami Divas.* Shay, Bali, and Evian still had stank attitudes about the way everything had gone down. (They claimed we'd had a pact to stick together and I sold them out by taking my own show. As if any of them would've turned it down if the shoe was on the other foot. Whatever.) Bali didn't even live in Miami anymore, and he still let me know he was mad with messy text messages, all of which I just ignored.

"So, do you know her or not?" Dexter asked again, snapping me out of my thoughts.

I knew he wasn't asking out of concern. He was probably trying to see if I could get some kind of inside scoop.

"Yeah, I know her. Or, at least I *used to* know her," I replied. "The Savannah I knew would never allow herself to look like that." I pointed at the screen.

"The research department is trying to see if we can find any other celeb arrests behind this drug," Dexter said.

I didn't get it because drugs were whack. Anything that took me off my A-game, I didn't need to be doing. And as fabulous as I was, I didn't need anything messing up my flaw-less bronze skin, long, all-natural, soft brown hair, and perfect Pilates-toned body. I was a quarter-piece (because a dime just didn't do me justice). So, no way would I ever let some kind of drug—be it weed, X, coke, or anything else—take that away from me.

Savannah used to be the same way. Was K2 powerful enough to make her change her mind? I glanced at the picture again. Obviously, it was, because Savannah had basically thrown her life away for it.

And that, I would never understand.

Chapter 2

I hadn't been able to get that picture of Savannah out of my head all night long. When I'd left the station after the show, I'd tried to call my friend Kirby. She and I used to take modeling classes with Savannah, and I knew the two of them talked regularly. I was hoping Kirby could tell me what was going on, but I hadn't been able to get in touch with her.

I glanced at my watch. Late again. Since I hadn't slept well, I was running late for school. (Oh, who was I kidding? I was always running late.) But this time I was later than normal. It was almost third period.

"Who's the fiercest chick at Miami High?" a voice from behind me said just as I entered the building.

I turned around and smiled at my BFF, Sheridan Matthews, looking her usual fly self in an orange Juicy Couture jacket and Rockstar jeans.

"Why, me, of course," we both said together, although I didn't have my usually *oomph*.

"What's up with you?" Sheridan asked, losing her smile. "You seem out of it."

"Just tired," I said.

"Me too," Sheridan replied, yawning as she got in step

with me. Sheridan was the daughter of the legendary Glenda Matthews, who was probably the hottest singer/actor in Hollywood. Ms. Matthews wanted to keep Sheridan away from the glitz of Hollywood, so she kept my BFF in Miami with some of their family, who were supposed to keep an eye on her. Notice I said *supposed to*, because those shiesty relatives just took Ms. Matthews's money and let Sheridan run free. That was perfectly fine with Sheridan, though. She loved not having to answer to anyone. Fortunately she had a good head on her shoulders and stayed out of trouble. Well, major trouble, anyway.

Sheridan and I walked past a group of students who were dragging up the walkway, late as well. Because of all the money our parents paid for us to go to the prestigious private Miami High School, the teachers often cut us slack when it came to things like punctuality, but I'd been pushing my luck since I'd started hosting *Rumor Central*. Not only was I late almost daily, my grades were plummeting because I barely had time for anything outside of the show. I'd been trying to get my academic act together since my mom had threatened to make me quit my show if I didn't get my grades up. (As if that would really happen.) Even still, I wasn't trying to flunk out of my senior year, so I'd been working on getting my grades up. There was nothing cute about being dumb.

I'd given up on the whole tutor thing because I hadn't had much luck with that. The last two tutors I'd had had turned out to be psychopaths (long story). Now I was just trying to do it myself.

"I know I look fabulous, and my body is here, but my mind is still snuggled up under my pillow," Sheridan said as we walked into the building just as the bell rang, dismissing the second period.

"Who are you telling?" I said. "It took everything under the sun for me to come to school today, but I have Mrs. Washington's test next. She said if I miss it I'll get a zero since it's a major grade, so here I am."

Sheridan stopped and stared at me. "Are you worried about your grade in her class? Is that why you look all stressed?"

I shook my head. My grades were concerning to me, but not enough to lose any sleep over. "Nah. Did you see the show yesterday? That's what's on my mind."

"Oh, yeah," Sheridan said, scooting out of the way as two of my silly classmates nearly knocked us over as they played in the hall. "Idiots!" Sheridan snapped, then turned back to me. "I tried to call you last night after I saw that. Is that the Savannah that you used to model with?"

I nodded. "Yeah, that's her. Wasn't that story wild?"

"Yeah, she looked horrible," Sheridan replied. "What happened to her?"

"What do you think happened? She got strung out, then she flipped out at a party. I haven't been able to get much more info than that." I was hoping that I could talk to Kirby sometime today because I really wanted to know what had happened to Savannah.

"I just can't believe it. I mean, didn't she just score that *Sports Illustrated* cover?" Sheridan asked.

"Umm-hmm," I replied. "But I'm sure they don't want her posing now." Savannah was just two years older than me, but she had already scored some gigs even seasoned models couldn't get. "Can you . . ." I stopped talking as my ex, Bryce Logan, walked toward me in the hallway. His arm was planted firmly around this girl named Callie, and she was giggling and smiling at him all dreamily. Yes, Bryce had money, looks, and physique. He was all that and then some. But, he was also history, which meant that he wouldn't be getting the time of day from me. I was all prepared to ignore him, but he tried to ignore me first.

Whatever. I just laughed as I opened my locker and pulled out my binder. The last thing I was going to do was give him any satisfaction that he was even on my radar.

"So that's how he's going to play it?" Sheridan asked,

turning her nose up at Bryce. He and Callie had stopped at
the end of the hallway and were kissing all over each other.
How tacky!

"He can play it however he wants," I replied, not looking
over his way even though I could see out of the corner of my
eye the way Callie was eyeballing me. "Bryce can have that
D-list chick." Bryce had been my boo. I'd thought he was my
soul mate, but we broke up because he let people fill his head
with a bunch of lies about me—twice. He tried to apologize,
but I didn't get down like that. If a guy was going to be with
me, he was going to be ride-or-die and nobody would be
able to tell him something about me to make him just dump
me (although I would never admit to anyone that Bryce had
actually dumped me and not the other way around).

"Yeah, he needs to know you've moved on anyway,"
Sheridan said, raising her voice so that Bryce could hear.

He didn't look up, but I could tell by the way his body
tensed up that he'd heard her.

Moved on? Not quite. J. Love, the R & B singer who had
just dropped yet another chart-topping hit, was still going
after me hard. And I had been tempted to give him some
play, but he'd dissed me, too. And although I may eventually
give him a second chance, he was going to have to work hard
for it, something he'd definitely been doing.

I glanced down at my diamond tennis bracelet, which
Sheridan quickly noticed. "Is that another gift from J. Love?"
she asked.

"Yep." I held up my wrist, revealing my ruby watch. "And
this is a gift from Alvin."

Sheridan was definitely impressed, but still she shook her
head. "Nice. But I don't know why you're wasting your time
with that nerd."

"Alvin is cool," I said. Alvin had helped me do some
computer stuff when I had been trying to track down this
crazed fan who was stalking me a few weeks before. And al-

though he'd ended up being a great guy, he was still too geeky for my taste. And Maya Morgan doesn't do nerds. Yes, I'd taken him to our winter dance, but that was about the extent of it. We talked on the phone almost every day and joked all the time. I really liked having him as a friend, but I didn't see it going any further than that.

"Must be hard being you." Sheridan laughed.

I didn't. "It is."

"Well, you can have your pick of guys. Alvin, J. Love, and I'm sure you could get Bryce back if you wanted."

"I don't," I said without hesitation. "That hoochie can have him."

"Well, I'm just saying. If you did want him, you could get him. J. Love wants you. Alvin wants you. Must be nice." I knew Sheridan was stressing because her boyfriend, Reginald, had moved away, and although lots of guys tried to holler at her (since she was almost as cute as me), none of them were on her level, so she was single and hating it.

"Nah, right now I'm just doing me," I said.

The show was keeping me busy. Digging up dirt and gossip on celebrities wasn't easy, and since I no longer ratted out my friends, I had to work even harder to get the scoop.

We stopped in front of my third-period classroom. "Well, let me get in this class and get ready for this stupid test. I'll talk to you later."

Sheridan waved, then bounced on to her class down the hall.

I walked in and slid in a desk near the back, where I usually sat. I looked at the empty seat in front of me, then leaned over to the girl who sat on the side of me.

"Hey, where's Lin?" I made it a point to sit behind Lin Vo because he was the smartest boy in the class and I might need to borrow some answers from him for today's test.

The girl—I didn't even know her name because she was

a scholarship student and didn't run in my circle—replied, "Girl, you haven't heard?"

"Heard what?" I wanted to add, "Dumbo," because if I'd heard where he was, I wouldn't have asked her.

"Lin got on some of that stuff."

"What stuff?"

"He got some bad Kush, apparently some kind of intensified Kush, and they had to rush him to the hospital. His brain is all jacked up," she said.

"What?" I asked in disbelief.

"Yeah, he . . ." She stopped talking when the teacher walked in and shot us be-quiet warning looks.

I was speechless anyway. Our celebrity circles were one thing. I knew sometimes things could get out of hand there, but if this drug was making its way to my classmates, it was a lot bigger than anyone might have ever thought!

Chapter 3

I was a little surprised to see my dad's car in the driveway when I made it home after school. He usually didn't get in until really late during the week. I knew my mom had her sorority executive board meeting and wouldn't be bothering me. So, I'd actually been looking forward to a quiet evening at home. I still hadn't caught up with Kirby, and wanted to try and do some digging myself to find out more about what had happened with Savannah.

But just as I was about to complain, images of this new Christian Dior dress I wanted popped in my head. Even though I had my own money, I'd much rather spend my dad's, so I'd been meaning to ask him to buy me the dress for this party I had coming up. Now would be the perfect time.

"Dad," I called out as I set my keys on the kitchen counter and dropped my messenger bag on the floor.

"Miss Maya," Sui said in a chastising tone. She gave me a stern look, then motioned toward the floor. I gave her a look right back.

"I asked you not to leave your bag in the floor," she said.

"Isn't that what we pay you for?" I glanced around the room. "Where's my dad?"

I could tell she wanted to say something, but she just gritted her teeth and said, "He's in the living room," as she bent down and picked my bag up off the floor.

I walked through our spacious kitchen and into the front room. "Dad . . ." I stopped in my tracks when I saw my dad—and the person standing in front of him. "Oh. My. God! Travis!" I raced over and threw my arms around my favorite cousin. "What are you doing here, boy?"

"Can you at least say hello?" he asked after hugging me. Travis stepped back from me and gave me the once-over. "Let me get a good look at you, girl. You ain't a little nerdy chick anymore," he said, turning me around.

I put my hand on my hip and cocked my head. "I was never a little nerdy chick, sweetie."

"My bad." He laughed. "You're right. You always were a diva."

"Hello, honey," my dad said, coming over and kissing me on the forehead.

"Hey, Dad." I turned right back to Travis. "What's going on? What are you doing here?"

Travis lived in Brooklyn, New York. I hadn't seen him since my grandfather's funeral last year. But up until then, we used to be "thick as thieves," as my grandfather used to like to say. We were close in age (he was only a few months older than me), and he was the brother I'd never had. Travis and I still talked via text, but I had always said that there was nothing like actually hanging out with him.

Travis didn't answer my question; instead, he just looked over at my dad.

"Where's Aunt Bev?" I asked. Aunt Bev was my dad's older sister and his only sibling. They weren't that close, but I just assumed it was because my dad was a workaholic and really didn't have time for anything but work.

"Well," my dad began, "we wanted to surprise you." My

dad patted Travis on the back. "Travis here is going to come stay with us for a while."

"What?" I exclaimed. "What do you mean, coming to stay with us?" I didn't know how I felt about that. Don't get me wrong. I loved Travis. He was definitely cool, but I hadn't shared my home—or my parents—with anyone, like ever.

"Just what he said," Travis replied. "I'm staying with you guys."

"Staying with us for what?"

"Oh, so you don't want me here?" he asked, a huge grin across his face. Travis had been a charmer for as long as I could remember, and it was that dimpled smile that usually did it.

"I'm just trying to find out what's going on," I replied.

"Oh, that's right. You're like a reporter. You go digging for answers."

"That's right," I replied. "And I'm not a reporter. I'm the star, baby."

Travis laughed as he plopped down on the sofa. "Yeah, I caught the show once or twice. I told everyone in Brooklyn you were my peeps. Nobody believed me though. I tried to call you, but your secretary wouldn't let me through."

"Whatever. You didn't try to call me," I said.

He smiled.

"In fact, I haven't heard from your janky behind except for your texts."

"Yeah, I just been a little busy."

My father cut his eyes at him. "Umm-hmmm, busy staying in trouble. But all that's about to change, right, son?"

"Yeah, Unc. I'm gonna be a regular Boy Scout." Travis held up his hand like he was taking some kind of oath.

"What kind of trouble you been getting into?"

"See, what had happened was . . ." He laughed. "Seriously, it wasn't even me. It was my boys. And Moms was tripping, talkin' about she can't handle me since my dad left."

"Yeah, but Uncle Myles can handle you. So don't get out of line," my dad said, pointing a warning finger at Travis.

Travis saluted him. "Yes, sir."

"I'm going to get back to work. You get settled in. Sui will show you to your room and get you situated. I have a friend who's giving me a great deal on a 2010 Camaro for you, so you'll have your own transportation."

At the mention of a car, Travis beamed. I couldn't help but frown. So, now we were buying him a car? But I decided not to trip. It wasn't like it was some luxurious car anyway.

"Who is Sui?" Travis asked.

"The maid," I replied. "Remember?"

"Dang, I forgot y'all were rolling like that. So what time is the chef preparing dinner?" He stood and walked back over to me.

"That's what I'm talking about," I said, laughing. "I've been trying to tell Dad that we need a personal chef."

"Sui cooks just fine," my dad called out as he headed into his study.

Travis stared at me a minute. I was used to that since I was all that, but it was creeping me out coming from a family member.

"Would you stop looking at me like that?"

"I'm just trippin' off you. You look like a little woman now."

"Whatever, boy."

He walked around the living room. My mom had actually remodeled since the last time he had been here. It had already been nice then, but she had gotten bored of the place we'd lived in since I was two. She'd knocked out a wall in the living room. Now, when you entered the foyer, it opened into a big rotunda and the living room sat to the left in a large, spacious area. Travis used to always say our living room looked like one of those homes in the magazines his mom drooled over. Whenever Aunt Bev used to visit, I remember she would get all teary-eyed like she was sad. My mom had told me it was because she was envious of her brother. Envious, but not jealous, my mother stressed, because "envious just meant that she wished she had what her brother had with no evil intent." Personally, both sounded like hatin' to me, but whatever.

"So, what's going on, lil cuz? You all big-time now." Travis beamed proudly. "I mean, you're kickin' butt and takin' names. I see your picture everywhere!"

"I'm just trying to do me." I tossed my hair over my shoulders. "Since no one else can."

"And I heard you were dating the singer J. Love."

"You heard wrong," I said, rolling my eyes and losing my smile.

"Okay, whatever you say." Travis grabbed his bag. "Show me to my portion of the castle."

I led the way upstairs and showed him to the guest room. He started unpacking. I looked at all his clothes, spread out on the bed. "Oooh, this is nice," I said, picking up a gold, heavy-duty watch.

He took the watch out of my hand. "Only thing I have worth something. And the only thing my dad ever gave me."

I didn't remember much about Travis's dad, except that he wasn't around.

"Oh, when did he give it to you?"

Travis tossed it back in a duffel bag. "Right before he left. I guess you can call it a parting gift. It's supposed to be worth a lot of money. I just been hanging on to it . . ." He paused. "Well, 'cause it's all I got left."

I remembered that talking about his dad always made him uncomfortable, so I changed the subject. "So for real, what you been getting into?" I asked as he put his suitcase up on the bed.

"Just trouble," he replied as he unzipped his suitcase and started removing baseball caps and all kinds of hip gear. "But I left the trouble back in Brooklyn. I'm starting over. So what time do we leave for school in the morning?"

"*We?*" I asked, sitting up straight. "What do you mean, 'we'?"

He flashed a big grin. "Yep. I'm the newest student at Miami High. You didn't think I was going to come here and not finish school, did you?"

"What? We're in the middle of the school year."

"And? You must've forgotten, my uncle is Myles Morgan. He pulled some strings and got them to find a spot for me." Travis walked over and started putting his stuff in the dresser drawers. He was setting up shop like he really was going to be here a while.

I wanted to ask him who was paying for his school since Aunt Bev didn't have the money, but of course, I knew the answer to that. My dad was footing that bill, which meant less money for me. I didn't know why Travis couldn't go to the public school down the street. All I knew was if my dad was shelling out money for Travis's tuition, I didn't want to hear anything when I asked for money.

As if he was reading my mind, Travis said, "Don't worry little cousin. I'm not going to be in the way. I'm just going to keep letting you do you."

I finally smiled. The more I thought about it, it might be nice to have my cousin around. I had my share of friends, but it would be nice to have some family around.

"Cool. As long as you don't forget it's only one star in the Morgan household," I said with my hands on my hips.

Travis grinned. "Believe me, I'm low-key. And I got a feeling, even if I did forget, you wouldn't hesitate to remind me."

"You got that right," I said as I stood and made my way out and back down to my father's study to convince him to give me money for my Christian Dior dress. So I readied my "I don't want to lose your love, Daddy, now that you have a boy" act. If that didn't get my four-thousand-dollar dress, nothing would.

Chapter 4

I was not ready for today. I loved my cousin, I really did, and I definitely loved kicking it with him. He was cool people. But too cool. Whenever Travis was around, he stole my shine. And I could tell today would be no exception.

"What's up?" he said, smiling at the two girls cheesing like he was some kind of superstar strutting across the parking lot. We had just arrived on campus and hadn't even made it inside the building when the girls started gawking.

"Heyyyy," the girls sang, giggling like they had had some kind of laughing gas or something.

I rolled my eyes. It was bad enough that I had to be up this early in order to get to school on time so we could get Travis settled in before first period; now I had to deal with all these thirsty chicks.

We had just rounded the corner when my classmates Zenobia and Angel eased up on the side of me.

"Well, hello, handsome," Zenobia said.

I knew this was going to be a problem. Travis was easily one of the hottest guys at Miami High now. He was Trey Songz fine, with smooth chocolate skin and a killer smile. Add to that the fact that he had a little bad-boy swag and a slamming personality, and I knew these chicks were going to be all over him.

Travis licked his lips and flirtatiously said, "Hello, pretty ladies."

"Hey," Angel said. I guess I was invisible or something.

"Excuse me," I said.

Zenobia turned to me and said, "So, Maya, do tell. Is this your new man?"

I turned up my lips. *As if.* "Number one," I said, folding my arms across my chest, not bothering to hide my attitude, "if he was my man, he wouldn't be licking his lips at you, flirting like some kind of hungry dog. This is my cousin, Travis. He just transferred here."

"Ooooh, *cousin,*" Zenobia sang. "So that means he's family."

"And fair game," Angel said, stepping closer to him. "Hi, Travis, I'm Angel." She stuck her hand out for him to shake. I wanted to tell him if he knew like I knew, he wouldn't touch her. Angel—with her oversized boobs and silicone-injected butt—was the biggest freak on campus. The only reason I even spoke to them was because both of them were stupid rich, which put them in the in-crowd by default.

Travis took Angel's hand and kissed it like he was in a Brad Pitt movie. I wanted to throw up.

"Angel? I can see why that's your name because you look like you just floated straight down from Heaven."

Oh my God. Talk about whack. "Are you for real?" I said, staring at my cousin. "Like, seriously?" I guess he was serious because he was grinning at Angel like she was the last biscuit at Sunday breakfast. "Boy, can you bring your corny behind on?" I said, grabbing him and pulling him off. "He'll see you around," I told Zenobia and Angel. "Or not."

"Bye, Travis," they sang.

He blew them kisses as he followed me. "So, what, you're my pimp now? You're regulating who I get to holla at?" He laughed. I know he was just playing around, but I didn't need any drama.

"Can you just get situated first before you go start breaking hearts?" I snapped, not breaking my stride as I headed to the front office. "I have a rep at this school, and I don't need these thirsty chicks mad because you're playing games."

"Oh, yeah, I forgot. My cuz is big stuff around here."

I stopped and turned to face him. "Yes, she is! And I don't need any unnecessary drama. *Comprende?*"

"Yeah, from what I hear, you do good at creating that all on your own." He giggled.

"Look, boy . . ." I waved a finger in his direction.

"Come on, Maya. You know I'm just messing with you," Travis said. He put his arm around my neck and pulled me into a hug.

I wiggled away from him. "Stop, and don't do that either."

"Oh, so now you got a problem with me hugging my little cousin?"

"And stop calling me little. You're only six months older than me," I corrected him. Yes, he was eighteen, but I would be, too, in six months. "I just don't need anyone thinking you're my man."

"Whatever." He looked around. "Where do I pick up my schedule?"

I huffed, then stomped off. We walked away while more girls stared, and some guys even sized him up, obviously trying to figure out who he was. I wanted to hang a sign around my neck that said, THIS IS NOT MY BOYFRIEND, but I just kept it moving.

We made our way to the front office. I showed Travis the counselor who had his schedule. He picked it up, and we headed to my locker just as the first bell rang. I couldn't remember the last time I had been at school for the first bell.

"Here, put this in there," Travis said, handing me the

notebook my mom had given him as we headed out this morning.

"Don't you need that?" I asked.

"For what? I get chicks to take notes for me." He actually popped his collar like some kind of pimp.

I rolled my eyes as I took the tablet and threw it in my locker.

"What classes do you have?" I asked.

He shrugged like he couldn't care less, then handed me his schedule as he scoped out the girls walking up and down the hall.

I was just about to say something about his schedule when Sheridan walked up. "Well, well, well. The rumors are true."

"What rumors?"

She ran her eyes up and down Travis's body. "The rumors that said Maya Morgan was sporting a new guy on her arm."

I groaned. "He's not a guy."

Travis cleared his throat, and this fool actually raised his shirt to show off his tight abs. "Last time I checked I was," he said. Of course, Sheridan and every other girl in a ten-foot radius started drooling.

"I mean, he's not *that* kind of guy," I told Sheridan. "This is just my cousin. You remember—Travis?"

Sheridan's mouth fell open. "Oh my God! Little Travis grew up." She pushed his shoulder. "How you gon' come to town and not let me know?"

We all used to hang out when Travis came down during the summers when we were in elementary school. But once he'd hit twelve, Travis hadn't been trying to come to Miami anymore. My dad had said he preferred to stay in Brooklyn and run the streets.

Travis looked at Sheridan and frowned like he was trying to figure out who she was. Finally he said, "Sheridan?"

"In the flesh, baby." She did a slow twirl.

"*Danggggg*," he slowly said. "Talk about growing up. You are so freakin' hot."

"Really, Travis?" I asked. I mean, my BFF was beautiful, but with her flat chest, I didn't know how she could ever be classified as hot.

"Wow, the last time I saw you, you had braces and crooked teeth," he said.

"I never had crooked teeth," she protested.

"Well, you definitely ain't no little awkward girl anymore. What happened to the little girl with pigtails I used to know?" Travis asked as he checked her out from head to toe.

"She grew up, too," Sheridan confidently replied.

"And out," he said, leaning back and looking at her behind.

"Now, you both are about to make me throw up in my mouth," I said. "What's your first class?" I said, glancing down at his schedule since it was obvious that was the least of his concerns.

Travis just kept staring at Sheridan.

"We do have one class together," I said, examining his schedule. "You have Mrs. McAfee first period."

"Oh, so you're in with me," Sheridan said, a huge smile forming across her face. "So I guess I'm going to have to take you under my wing and show you the ropes."

"That ain't the only thing I want to get under," he muttered.

"Travis!"

"My bad." He stepped back and threw his hands up like he was surrendering. "My cousin here got me on lockdown. I got a no-chick rule. I can't talk to any girls today."

"And he can't talk to *you* any day," I quickly added.

Travis shrugged. "The pimp has spoken."

Sheridan rolled her eyes. "Maya, stop being so extra."

"Whatever," I replied. I wasn't about to debate this with

them. The bell had already run, and since it wasn't often that I made it to school this early, I wanted to at least get to first period on time. "Travis. Come on, I'll show you where your class is."

"What kind of sense does that make?" Sheridan said. "We have the class together. I might as well show him."

"I can think of a whole lot of things you can show me," Travis said, causing Sheridan to break into a big, stupid grin.

"I'm warning you guys . . ." They may have been just playing around, but I needed them both to know that their hooking up was *not* an option.

"Chill out, it's not even like that," Sheridan said. "You're like my sister, right? Well, that would make Travis my cousin, too." She draped her arm through his. "So, come on, cuz. Let me show you to class."

I shook my head as I watched them walk away. I hadn't seen Travis in a while, but one thing I did know, my cousin was a player. My gut told me if he and Sheridan hooked up, my BFF would be the one getting played.

Chapter 5

"You are so full of it."

I took a deep breath, folded my arms across my chest and gave Bryce major attitude. I couldn't believe he was standing here in my face. We hadn't really talked since our last break-up. I'd never let on how much that had hurt me, but Bryce was old news so he would get no more of my time.

"Is there a reason you're invading my personal space?" I asked him. He'd been waiting outside my fifth-period class like some kind of stalker.

Bryce let out a small laugh, almost like he was mocking me. "Naw, I'm just trippin' on you. I can't believe you're tryin' to act all funky about me and Callie."

Was he really coming at me like this? I debated telling him off, but I didn't even have the energy. "Really, Bryce? I couldn't care less about you and Callie."

"Whatever. I saw the way you were looking at us the other day. Then you had your girl make that comment." He had the nerve to try and look cocky like he'd caught me in a lie. He was seriously delusional because Sheridan may have been paying him attention, but he wasn't even on my radar.

"What do you want, Bryce?" I asked.

He hesitated, then said, "I'm just trippin' because I see you all hugged up with a new dude, but you want to give me grief."

I pointed my finger in his face. "First of all, nobody is giving you grief. Do you, boo. What part of 'I am completely cool on you' do you not get?" I didn't wait for him to answer. "And number two, what are you talking about? Hugged up with who?"

"Ol' boy that you gave a ride to school the other day." He shook his head like I was pathetic. "You can't get a dude with his own ride?"

I couldn't help it—I busted out laughing in Bryce's face. "What, you stalking me now? You spying on me?" I asked him. Bryce had always been the jealous type. I imagined him sitting up watching me with Travis, and burning up inside with envy. That brought another smile to my face.

"Ain't nobody spying on you," Bryce protested. "I just happened to see you when you rolled up with that buster sitting on the passenger side. Then, you walking around all hugged up with him."

Hugged up? Then, I remembered when Travis had playfully hugged me and I'd pushed him off. Oh, Bryce was so off base it was funny.

I almost came clean, but why give Bryce the satisfaction? Let him think whatever he wanted. I no longer cared because Bryce was no longer my problem. "If only you knew." I looked him up and down. "But you don't."

I wasn't going to waste any more of my precious brain cells thinking about Bryce. He'd blown his chance with me. He'd find out sooner or later that Travis was just my cousin, but for now, let him think what he wanted. In fact, I kinda wished Travis were here now. He would have played right along and helped me drive Bryce crazy.

Bryce had me worked up as I got in my car and headed home so I did what I usually did when I was in a bad mood. I called Alvin.

I'd first met Alvin a few weeks ago when my other BFF, Kennedi, put me in touch with him so he could help me figure out who was hacking into my email account. Alvin was some kind of computer whiz (he even made a lot of money off one of his computer inventions). And although he could be cute if somebody took some of that money and cleaned him up, he wasn't in my league.

I knew Alvin wanted more with me, but he was a nerd with a capital N. He was a rich nerd, but he was a nerd nonetheless, so we could never really be anything but friends. But over the past couple of months, we'd gotten to be really good friends. We talked almost every day. Alvin had a great sense of humor and he had a knack for making me laugh. After my encounter with Bryce, I definitely felt like laughing.

I was about to dial his number when my phone died. "Dang it," I said, looking around for my car charger. Then I remembered that Travis had pulled the plug out and taken it inside at school so he could charge his phone. I tossed my dead phone on the seat as I wondered where he was. He'd just told me at sixth period that he had another way home. When I asked him how, he said one of his friends was coming through to pick him up. Leave it to my cousin to make friends that fast.

I got on the freeway, and was just about to head home, when I decided to make a right and go by Alvin's instead. I was off today and I needed some laughter to pull me out of my funk (before Bryce had come trippin' with me, I'd found out I had flunked yet another test). Alvin was just the man to cheer me up. I smiled as I thought about the first time Alvin and I had really hung out, at our winter dance. J. Love had tried to punk him there. Alvin had showed me then that he wasn't one to be messed with. One day, he was going to make some girl a good boyfriend. If he ever got out of the house long enough to go meet someone.

I pulled into the driveway of Alvin's spacious four-bedroom house. At first, I hadn't been feeling Alvin (who is twenty-one) living at home with his parents, but then, he'd explained that it was *his* house and his mom lived with him.

I parked and made my way up to the front door. I rang the doorbell and waited a few minutes until I saw Alvin pull the curtain back over the little window on the door. I waved. It took a minute, but Alvin slowly opened the door.

"Hey," he slowly said.

"Hey, yourself," I replied. "What's up?"

"Nothing. Ummm, what are you doing here?"

"I was just on my way home and decided to swing by."

The look on his face actually made me lose my smile because I wasn't missing the fact that he hadn't moved from the crack in the front door.

"Are you going to let me in?" I finally asked.

Alvin hesitated, then said, "It's just that . . ."

"Move, boy." I pushed him aside and walked in. I had no idea why he was acting all secretive, but I wanted to get inside. "Why are you . . ." I stopped in my tracks at the sight of the pretty girl with olive skin sitting on Alvin's sofa. She looked like a young Jennifer Lopez. She had on a low-cut blouse, which she was buttoning up as I walked in.

"Wow," I said, looking back and forth between him and the girl. "Just wow."

Alvin scooted to her side as she stood up. "Hey, Marisol, ummm, this is ah, ah, ah . . ."

I cocked my head, raising an eyebrow in his direction. *Is he for real?* "Um, Maya. My name is Maya."

"Don't be silly, girl, I know your name," he said with an I'm-so-in-trouble laugh.

Marisol had an expression on her face like she wasn't sure if some drama was about to jump off.

"Hi, nice to meet you," she said, sticking her hand out.

Alvin jumped over to her side. "Marisol is a friend of mine," he quickly said. It was then that I noticed he was wearing a cute purple polo and some baggy jeans. This was a shock because I don't think I'd ever seen him not in a button-down shirt and slacks.

I looked over at Marisol as she pulled her shirt down, then quietly looked up at me, then at Alvin. I was glaring at him, and he was looking at me like he didn't know what to do.

"Do I need to leave?" Marisol finally asked.

"That's probably a good idea," I said.

"Maya!" Alvin repeated.

I shrugged as I folded my arms across my chest. "No, I just figured she had to get home or something." My eyes roamed down to her too-tight shirt and too-short skirt. "You know, and find some clothes that fit."

"Maya!" Alvin said. "Why are you acting like that?"

"Alvin, what's going on?" Marisol said, looking she was about to get upset.

I had to catch myself. I was for real tripping. I was acting like Alvin was my man. "No, I'm really just a friend," I told her. "I mean, he can't even remember my name so I must not be too important," I couldn't help but add.

"Come on, Maya. Stop tripping," Alvin said.

"Seriously, it's all good." I fake smiled at her. "We're just friends. I didn't mean to interrupt what you guys had going on over here."

"Maya, it's no big deal," Alvin said. "Marisol and I were just hanging out."

"Oh, okay then," I said, walking over and sitting down on the sofa. "In that case, what y'all talking about?" I crossed my legs like I was getting comfortable.

Alvin shot me a look like he couldn't believe me. I couldn't believe me either. I was feeling some kind of way. In the entire time I'd known him, I'd never known Alvin to go out on a date—let alone be sitting up making out with some chick. Then, I didn't know what bothered me more, that or how flustered he'd gotten when I'd showed up. If it truly was nothing, why was he so nervous?

"Wait a minute," Marisol said as she leaned in and stared closer at me. "Are you that girl from the TV show, the gossip show?"

"Yep, I'm that girl," I said with confidence.

"Oh, wow. I love that show," she said excitedly. "I mean, I could never do what you do."

"I'm sure you couldn't."

"I mean I couldn't sell my friends out like that. But you do a good job at it."

I just stared at her, trying to see if she was taking a dig at me on purpose or if she really was that dense.

"So, you just stopped by?" Alvin asked, standing over me.

"Yes. Me dropping by has never been a problem before." I didn't bother trying to hide my attitude.

"It's n-not one now," he stammered. "I was just saying, I mean, I didn't . . ."

"It's okay, *papi*," Marisol said, draping her arms through his. "I don't mind sharing you."

Now, I knew I was going to throw up. "On second thought, I just remembered something I need to do." I stood up. "*Papi*, I'll call you later," I said, sarcastically. "Bye, Pine-Sol."

She gritted her teeth, but kept her smile. "It's *Marisol*."

"Oh, my bad."

Alvin gently pushed me toward the door. Once he opened it, he stepped outside with me. "Why are you acting like that? Are you mad at me or something?"

I had to take a deep breath. Like, seriously, why was I tripping? We were just friends, and Alvin was a good guy. Why didn't I want him to be happy?

"No," I finally said. "You know I'm just messing with you." I couldn't help it—I ran my finger along the collar of his polo. "I'm glad to see you happy. But honestly, I think you can do better than that trashy girl. But hey, that's just me."

"Of course, you'd think that."

"I'm just looking out for your best interest," I said innocently.

"I know." He leaned in and kissed me on the cheek. "You don't want me, but you don't want anyone else to have me either. I get it. I'll call you later."

I just smiled because I was beginning to think there was some truth to what he was saying. "You do that, *papi*. Call me later." I made my way to my car, still struggling to make sense of the strange, bubbling feeling in my stomach.

Chapter 6

The newsroom of WSVV was a flurry of activity. Reporters, producers, and interns were running around like crazy.

"Where's the fire?" I asked Sonnie, one of the news producers, as I walked up to the main desk. I didn't usually make my way to this side of the building, but I'd finally gotten in touch with Savannah. She was in rehab now and had agreed to give me an interview when she got out. So, I'd left school right after lunch and come into the office to try and dig up some background info on other designer drug cases.

"Girl, it's a middle school that has had seven kids overdose," she said, scribbling furiously on a sheet of paper. Before I could reply, the desk phone rang. "Hey, this is the police department calling back," she yelled to no one in particular before snatching the phone up.

"Wow." I was grateful I worked on the entertainment side. I was only doing the drug stories as it pertained to celebrities. The idea of having to deal with that kind of stuff day in and day out, I definitely wasn't feeling.

"I guess I'll just come back," I mouthed to Sonnie, who had the phone nestled between her shoulder and her ear.

"Yeah, this is major so I'm not going to be able to get anyone to help you for a while."

"Cool," I replied.

I had just turned to walk away when I heard her say, "Oh no, so four of the kids have died?" she said.

I couldn't take any more. The news side was so freaking depressing. I made my way out of the newsroom before they completely ruined my day.

I had just sat down at my desk when my boss, Tamara, knocked on my door.

"Hey, Maya. Lynn from news wants to know if you have any contact information for Chanel Jackson."

"The actress?" I asked.

"Yeah, apparently, her little sister is one of the middle school kids that overdosed."

I leaned back in my chair. "Wow, this stuff is out of control. I just left the news department and it's chaos."

"Yeah, tell me about it. We got a tip today on another celebrity. I just don't get it. This K2 is supposed to be the cheap stuff, so why are all these rich people indulging in it?"

I shrugged. I had long ago stopped trying to figure out druggies.

"I don't know Chanel, but I can try to make some calls," I said.

"I appreciate it. They have your story for today lined up." She pointed to the folder on my desk. I picked it up and began sifting through it. Of course, we were reporting another K2 story. I had an eerie feeling that things with this drug were about to get even more out of control.

My cell phone rang as I was reading over everything. It was my mom.

"Hey, Mom," I said, answering. "I can't talk long. I'm about to go on the air."

I still had two hours before taping, but the last thing I felt like doing was sitting up on the phone with my mother.

"Hey, sweetie. You could at least say 'how are you, Mother?' "

I sighed and rolled my eyes. "How are you, Mother?"

"Thank you. That's much better. I'm fine. Your father wanted me to check and see how things are going with Travis since neither of you has bothered to let us know."

I wanted to ask my mom if she didn't have some charitable or community work to concern herself with, but instead I said, "Sorry. Things were hectic yesterday, but he got situated fine." I looked at my watch. It was now four o'clock. "Why didn't you just go ask him?"

"Because he's not here," she replied.

"What do you mean, he's not there?" He should've been home by now. He didn't get his car until next week so I didn't know where he could've gone, unless he hooked up with his friend again.

"Just what I said," my mother continued. "I got in about fifteen minutes ago and he wasn't here."

"Let me call him," I said. "I'll call you back."

My mom had barely hung up before I was punching in Travis's number. It went straight to voice mail.

I brushed away thoughts of my cousin. I had too much work to do. I wasn't about to babysit him. He was a big boy, and he'd make his way home soon enough.

Chapter 7

I didn't know why, but I wanted to hang out with my cousin. I'd scored my Savannah interview, and Travis had spent the week making up for being such a pain. He'd turned back into the old Travis, keeping me in stitches because he was always cracking jokes. That's why, when I finished taping the show, I hightailed it home to hang out with him. I'd changed out of my work clothes and into some comfortable leggings and a tank top and was making my way down the hall to Travis's room. He'd gotten his car, hooked up with one of his boys, and been on the move all week. But today, we were hanging out—whether he wanted to or not.

I was just about to knock on his closed bedroom door when I heard him say, "Come on, stop crying, Ma."

Instinct made me pause my knock midair and lean in a little closer. (What? I'm nosey. I don't try to make a secret of it.)

"Mama, please stop crying," Travis begged. He paused, then said, "You need to ask Uncle Myles to pay for the surgery. Why don't you let me ask Uncle Myles?" Another pause. "Okay, fine. I won't ask. But that's just crazy. That's your brother. . . . So what are you going to do about your medication then? I can't believe they expect someone with no insurance to pay three hundred dollars for some pills. . . . Okay, whatever. Can you get Mrs. Winston next door to take you down to Western Union? I'll send you the money for your pills. . . . Don't worry about it. I got it handled. I'll get the money. . . . No, Ma. I got a job."

I raised an eyebrow. That was news to me. In the past week, Travis had gone to school and come home. He'd hooked up with some of his friends, but as far as I knew, he hadn't gotten a job.

"Okay . . . I love you, Ma. Try to get some rest. You kicked me out so you wouldn't be stressed out and you're still stressed out. . . . Okay, okay. I'm kidding. I know you didn't kick me out. Just rest, okay? I love you. Bye."

I waited a few minutes, then knocked. "Hey, what's up?" he asked after telling me to come in.

"Nothing. Just seeing what you were up to." I had a million questions swirling through my head. What was wrong with Aunt Bev? Why didn't she want him to ask my dad for help? I wanted to know what kind of job he had. But from the look on his face I knew he wouldn't tell me the truth anyway. So, I just tried to steer the conversation in a general area.

"So, how are you liking it here?"

"It's cool. This"—Travis motioned around his oversized bedroom—"takes some getting used to. Shoot, our whole apartment could fit right in this room."

Like me, Travis was an only child. He did have an older brother who died when we were seven. Terrance had been a part of a gang and had died in some kind of retaliation shooting. I'm sure that's why Aunt Bev wanted Travis to leave New York. I didn't understand why she just didn't move. No way would I live in some place where I was scared to go to sleep at night.

I plopped down across his bed. "So, what was it like growing up in the ghetto? Did you live in one of those tall, crime-ridden, rundown buildings?"

Travis spun around in his chair and laughed. "You've been watching too many episodes of *Good Times*."

I frowned. "Ugh, I don't watch that show."

"Well, it was hard living." Travis smiled like he was recalling some good memories. "But it was home. Me and my moms and my friends, we may not have had much, but we had each other. I mean, I know that sounds like some corny greeting-card stuff, but it's the truth."

"So, you're in a gang?"

"Nah. After what happened to Terrance, I would've given my mom a heart attack if I'd gotten caught up in a gang. We had basketball, so the gangs left us alone."

"What happened with you and basketball?"

He shrugged sadly. "Got kicked off the team."

"Where's your dad?" I remembered my mom and dad talking about how he'd just up and left when Travis was a little boy.

Travis shook his head. "Your guess is as good as mine."

An empty silence hung in the room until I said, "So what kind of trouble have you been getting into?" I asked.

"Look, girl, you interviewing me for your TV show? If so, you need to be paying me." He held his hand out and rubbed his fingers together. I ignored him and kept talking.

"What about girls? You got a girlfriend back at home?"

That made him smile. "You know I got some shorties I've been hanging with, but Brooklyn is a long way and I knew y'all had all those *mamacitas* down here, so I had to let all the New York girlfriends go."

"Umph. Girlfriends, plural, huh? Yeah, I bet you were breakin' hearts left and right."

"Nah, it ain't even like that. I was trying to start fresh. Stay out of trouble, ya know?"

"What do you mean, was?"

He had this look like I'd caught him or something, but then he quickly recovered. "I'm just sayin'. I'm just trying to make my moms proud."

Just then, the doorbell rang. I pulled out my phone and punched the app that accessed our security monitor. I pushed the camera button and saw who was at the gate.

"What is Sheridan doing here?" I mumbled as I punched the key to open the gate. I jumped up from the bed and went down to meet her at the door.

"What's up?" I said, opening the door just as she came up the walkway.

"Nothing," she said, smiling. "Just thought I'd drop by and see what you were up to."

I frowned. Sheridan didn't usually just drop by. Then, when I looked at the way she was goggling at Travis, who had appeared in the doorway behind me, I said, "Unh-unh. I told y'all. Not happening."

Sheridan laughed as she pushed me out of the way and walked inside. "Girl, please. You said you were off. I just came to hang."

Travis smiled as she pointed to the sofa. "Make yourself comfortable. We weren't doing anything."

Something didn't feel right, and I was about to call them on it when my phone rang. I glanced at them, then turned my attention to my phone. The number was from the station.

I punched the talk button. "Hello."

"Hey, Maya, where are you?" my executive producer, Tamara, asked.

"I'm at home."

"You know the kids who had the drugs yesterday? One of the girls is brain-dead."

"What? She was like fourteen years old."

"Look, her friends who were getting high with her want to

talk to *Rumor Central*. Now." Tamara had on her no-nonsense voice.

"Now?"

"Yeah, they'll be at the station in an hour and a half. Can you get here?"

I paused as I glanced over at Travis and Sheridan, who were sitting on the sofa giggling and whispering.

"Well, I was just about to—"

"Look, Maya," Tamara said, cutting me off, "if you can't do it, just say so. I'll try to find someone else."

Images of the last girl who'd tried to take my job—my former assistant, Ariel—flashed through my mind. My position as host of *Rumor Central* was a hot one, and I constantly had to watch my back from people trying to take me off my throne.

"Nah, it's cool," I finally told her. "I'm on my way."

"Good," Tamara replied like she'd had no doubt I would come. "When you get in, go straight to hair and makeup. I'll make sure all the details are waiting on you. See you in a bit." She quickly hung up the phone before I could say anything else. I sighed, then turned to Travis and Sheridan.

"I just got called into work, major story." I pointed to Sheridan. "You gonna roll out with me?"

Travis spoke up before she could respond. "No, she can stay and watch a movie with me."

"Yeah," Sheridan said. "You're the superstar, not me. So I'm just gonna chill and watch a movie with Travis. I've been dying to see this movie."

I looked at her like she was stone-cold crazy. "You've been dying to see *Batman*?"

"Actually, it's *The Dark Knight*," Travis corrected.

I tsked. "Sheridan doesn't even like movies like that." I put my hands on my hips. "And I don't think it's a good idea to be leaving her here alone with you."

"Maya would you chill? We're just watching a stupid movie."

I looked back and forth between the two of them. Sheridan had a stupid look on her face.

"We're in your parents' house. What do you think is gonna happen?" Travis said.

"Besides, it's not even like that," Sheridan added.

I relaxed a bit. "Okay, fine. Travis, tell my mom I got called in." I ran upstairs to change, but I swear, it looked like the two of them were happy to be alone.

Chapter 8

It had been a long day at school and I was just glad the day was over. I was starving and in the mood for something I very seldom had—a big fat, greasy burger. I didn't indulge in junk food (the cameras weren't kind to big girls), but today, Smashburger was calling my name.

"Sheridan," I said, catching up with her at her locker right after the last bell rang. "What are you about to do?"

"Nothing."

"I am starving. Let's go get something to eat."

"Ummm," she stammered, her eyes suddenly darting up and down the hall like she was on the lookout for someone.

"What's wrong with you?" I asked.

"N-nothing."

I was too hungry to try and figure out why she was acting strange. "Well, did you hear me? I said, let's go get a burger. My treat."

"I can't go," she said hurriedly. "I just remembered I have something to do."

"But you just said you weren't doing anything."

"I know, but ummm, I forgot about something I was supposed to be doing right after school."

"What's wrong with you?" I studied her for a minute. She was acting really strange.

"Nothing. I just have a lot of stuff on my mind."

"Fine, whatever," I said, throwing my book into my locker. I had just closed it when Travis walked up. "What's up, cuz?" I said, turning to him. I was so hungry, I'd treat him to something to eat. "Sheridan is too busy for me, so it's me and you. Let's go get something to eat."

"Well, ah, actually—" he said, glancing over at Sheridan, who immediately looked down. "Actually, we were about to go—" Sheridan gave him a look, and he stopped talking mid-sentence.

I folded my arms across my chest. "About to do what?"

"Nothing." Sheridan immediately jumped in the middle of our conversation. "We weren't about to do anything."

"Girl, please." Travis grabbed Sheridan and pulled her toward him. "Maya ain't my mama. Me and Sheridan 'bout to roll out and get something to eat."

"Roll out?" I said, confused. "Like together?"

Neither of them said a word so I said, "So, what, y'all an item now?"

"Yep," Travis said confidently.

"You've been here all of two weeks and now you're hooking up with my best friend. Although I should probably say *former* best friend since my BFF didn't see fit to tell me she was getting with my cousin."

Sheridan took a step toward me. "Come on, don't be like that," she said. "I just knew you would be trippin' if you knew."

"You were right about that," I snapped.

"You're more than welcome to come with us," Sheridan said, trying a flash a fake smile. She knew I was pissed. I didn't want the two of them hooking up because when Travis broke her heart, I didn't need her getting mad at me.

"I don't believe this."

"Come with us, Maya," she said.

I shook my head. "Nah, I don't do third wheels so enjoy your date." I threw my hands up as I walked off.

I had just made it to the corner in the hallway when I heard, "Is Maya being dumped by her BFF?"

I turned to see Shay and her group of hyena girlfriends standing around, gawking.

"Umph, it looks like there's trouble in paradise," added Chenoa, one of the cheerleaders I'd exposed in a story last year.

"Hey, Chenoa, you still in the trickin' business?" I asked. She took a step toward me. I wanted to tell her don't go there with me because I wasn't in the mood.

Chenoa and a few of her fellow cheerleaders had actually run an escort service out of Miami High. It had been one of the first stories I'd done on *Rumor Central*, and she hadn't been able to stand me ever since then. I don't know why, since Daddy Dearest had gotten her off. But my story had also shut down their little side hustle.

Of course Shay would hang out with anyone who hated me. Shay was ghetto royalty. Her dad played for the Miami Heat—well, when he wasn't on suspension for fighting, drug use, and everything else. I would give it to him, though—he was one of the best in the league, which was why he still had a contract.

"What's up, Maya? How's the show going?" Shay asked, fake as all get-out.

"You don't watch?" I asked. I had to bite my tongue, because I was about to tell her she might want to watch and take some notes on how to be fab on TV, something she obviously didn't know since she was one of the ones they'd cut from our show, *Miami Divas*. But I had tried to make peace with her because I'd needed her help last month when I had been trying to catch someone who had hacked into my email account. We would never be cool like that, but I didn't need any unnecessary drama so I left it alone.

"Nah, I don't watch. I can't seem to find time to fit it in my schedule," Shay said nonchalantly.

"Do you need some friends?" Chenoa asked in a baby voice. I just wanted to pop her in her eye.

"Nah, I'm good in the friend department," I told her.

They glanced over at Sheridan, who was giggling as Travis whispered something in her ear.

"I heard you didn't even know they'd hooked up," Chenoa said. "I knew. We all did."

Several of the girls nodded. They all made me sick. "Well, good for all of you. I really have more important things to do than worry about who anyone is getting with."

"Do you really?" Chenoa said. "I thought that's how you got famous, getting all up in someone else's business."

"Whatever," I said, turning to walk off. I just needed to ignore all of them.

As I made my way out to my car, I glanced over my shoulder at Travis and Sheridan. They were acting like two lovesick lovebirds. I didn't know what had me angrier, the fact that everyone at school had known they had hooked up and I hadn't, or the fact that they'd hooked up, period.

I wanted to tell Sheridan that when my cousin left her on the side of the road in tears, she couldn't come crying to me. But I knew my BFF—she was going to have to learn the hard way.

Chapter 9

Okay, enough was enough. I'd been ignoring Alvin's calls and his texts. He'd even tweeted a picture of a doghouse and a message that said, Can I come out? It was funny, but I still wouldn't take his call. The whole not-remembering-my-name thing was so not cool. But I'd made him suffer long enough. So, I picked up the phone and punched in his number.

"Hello?" he answered on the second ring.

"Hey," I said.

"Maya." He sounded relieved to hear from me.

"How are you?" I definitely wanted to play it like nothing was wrong.

He was treading lightly. I guess he was trying to see if I was still angry. "I'm cool. So glad to finally hear from you," he said.

"What you doing?" I said, casually.

I heard rustling, like he was walking, then he said, "Nothing, I was just chilling." It now sounded like I heard an echo, like he had stepped into a bathroom or something.

"Where are you?"

He paused, then said, "Ummm, I was just out getting something to eat."

"Oh. Are you alone?" The words came out before I even realized it.

Alvin was quiet, and then I heard, "Hey, *papi,* is everything okay?"

And once again, it felt like someone had hit me in the stomach.

"I guess that answers my question," I said.

"Nah, me and Marisol just came to get something to eat. That's all," Alvin said, but I could definitely tell he had lowered his voice.

"Whatever, Alvin."

"Maya, if it was that serious, I wouldn't have even answered your call."

"Oh, so now you're doing me a favor by taking my calls?"

"You know I didn't even mean it like that."

"No, you know what, I'm just going to let you go on back to your date and I'm going to talk to you later." I quickly hung up, then tossed my phone on the sofa next to me. I sat there, fuming and trying to figure out why the heck I was so bothered about who Alvin was kickin' it with. It wasn't like I wanted him, so what was with the crappy feeling in my stomach?

I tried to forget that conversation as I began quickly turning the pages of my magazine. I was taking my frustrations out on *People.*

"So, are you still salty with me?"

I looked up to see Travis standing over me, and I couldn't help but roll my eyes. I didn't say a word and just kept flipping through the magazine. I had a rare day off and I was stretched out across the living room sofa watching our seventy-two-inch TV and reading my magazine.

Yes, I was still mad at him. And Sheridan. But I'd called her anyway to talk about Alvin and that skank hadn't even called me back. I guess she was too busy kicking it with my cousin. Well, that was why I didn't have anything to say to her or to him.

"I'm going to take that as a yes," Travis said, plopping down on the sofa next to me when I didn't answer.

Travis had been here less than three weeks and had already stolen some of my shine and taken over my best friend. Thank God Kennedi was coming here this weekend. Travis and Sheridan could go jump off a bridge for all I cared. I made a memo to myself to keep Kennedi far away from Travis before he stole her, too.

"Come on, Maya. Don't be like that," Travis said. "We try to invite you along, but you always trippin'."

"I told you, I'm not about to be a third wheel," I huffed. "So go do you."

"Well, let me fix you up with my boy. Then, we could all go out together." He smiled like he'd just come up with the most brilliant plan ever.

"Boy, please," I said. "I don't need anyone fixing me up with anyone."

"Seriously, I think you'll like him. You guys would have a lot of fun together. He's like me."

"What, a liar?"

Travis didn't seem fazed by my insult. "No, he's fun, and good looking."

"Why are you bothering me?" I said, cutting him off. "I'm sure you have a date or something."

Travis ignored me as he put his feet up on the table. I looked at him like he was crazy. "Ummm, that's a twelve-thousand-dollar imported Egyptian marble table. You must want to die a slow and painful death at the hands of my mom," I said, pointing at his feet.

He dropped his feet but kept talking. "You know, I figured the best thing to make you feel better about kicking it with us was if you had a date of your own."

That actually made me close my magazine. "I don't know

how many ways to tell you this. I don't need you fixing me up with anyone. Maya Morgan doesn't do blind dates. You won't have me sitting up with some dork."

"Nah, this dude is cool people," Travis said. "I mean, I don't think you should be getting serious or anything, but he's someone great to hang out with."

"Whatever, Travis. Go somewhere with that."

He smiled as he stared me up and down.

"Why are you staring at me like that?"

"I'm just making sure you look together."

"I always look together," I told him.

"Well, you know, first impressions are everything so I just wanted to make sure you were tight."

I sighed. "What are you talking about, Travis?"

Just then, the doorbell rang. My cousin jumped up before I could say anything.

"Who is that?" I asked, getting up and following him.

"Oh, just a friend." Travis opened the door. "What's up, man?" He gave a brotherly hug to the guy standing on the other side of the door. Or should I say *the model*, because this guy standing on my doorstep looked like he had just stepped off the runway. He looked like a darker, much younger version of that actor Boris Kodjoe. In fact, he looked like he could be Boris's little brother.

"It's all you," the guy said, walking in. I tried not to stare. I would never tell Travis, but my cousin was handsome. But this guy, he put Travis to shame.

"Yo, this is my cousin I was telling you about," Travis said, pointing at me. "Maya, this is my boy, Sammy Martin."

I hesitated before finally shaking his hand. Sammy was fine and all, but I still wasn't feeling a blind date. I didn't need him thinking I was some kind of desperate chick who couldn't get her own date.

"Well, I'm gonna let you two handle your business," I said, turning to leave.

Sammy kinda looked sideways at Travis.

"Maya, what you doin'?" Travis said. "I told you I had someone coming over."

"I hope you didn't invite him over here for me," I said. "I told you, I don't do blind dates."

Sammy held up his hands. "Whoa. Hey, it isn't even like that. No hard feelings," he said with a warm smile. "I don't believe in having any chick kick it with me that doesn't want to be there." He side-eyed Travis. "I thought this was all cool. My apologies," he said, before turning around and heading to the door.

Travis gave me a look, and I felt frozen for a minute. Had Sammy just dismissed me? *No,* I said to myself as I shook that thought off. I'd told him that I wasn't interested, and obviously, Sammy wasn't the type to play around.

"Wait," I said, just as he reached the door. I walked over to him. "Sorry, didn't mean to be such a jerk, but my cousin here could've given me a little warning."

"I did," Travis protested.

"Yeah, but you could've told me before two minutes ago." I faced Sammy. "But it's all good. Come on in. Would you like something to drink?"

"Nah, I was actually hoping to take you somewhere nice," he said. "I even made reservations at that new seafood restaurant down on South Beach."

I couldn't help but smile. That place was the new hot spot, but it cost a grip for a meal. So, if Sammy had taken it upon himself to make reservations there, that meant he couldn't be half bad. Images of my failed relationships with Bryce and J. Love, and even Alvin and Marisol, flashed through my head.

No, maybe Sammy Martin might be exactly what I needed.

Chapter 10

I had dated my share of guys who could hold their own—Bryce (the son of an NFLer), J. Love (the singer), my first boyfriend (a model)—and Sammy was ranking right up there with them. It didn't take but a couple of minutes for me to realize that Sammy truly had it going on. Last night, it had been dinner at the exclusive South Beach restaurant. Tonight, we were going to a VIP reception that even I hadn't been invited to. Don't ask me how he'd gotten the tickets. When I asked him, he just smiled and told me, "Don't worry about it."

I was in my bedroom getting dressed like some kind of giddy chick who had never been anywhere. Sammy had told me to just look my usual gorgeous self and not worry about what time he was coming or any other details of the night. Usually, I didn't take too kindly to guys trying to boss me around, but I was feeling him, so I let him make it.

I saw Sammy pull up outside. I quickly punched in the security code to the gate. I raced toward the door. "I'm gone," I yelled out to my parents, who were sitting in the kitchen, talking.

"Where are you going?" my mom shouted back.

"On a date!"

"With whom? Where?" she yelled, but I pretended I didn't hear her.

I had just reached the car when Sammy got out. "What are you doing?" I asked. "Let's go."

"Slow your roll," he replied. "Are your parents home?"

I stared at him like he'd lost his mind. "My parents? Yeah, why?"

He shut his door and began walking up the sidewalk. "I'm not about to just swing through here and grab you without saying something to them. That's disrespectful."

My mouth was open. Was he for real? "Boy, if you don't quit playing and come on . . ." I opened his car door, but he kept walking.

"I don't believe this," I muttered as I turned and followed him.

Just as he reached the front door, it swung open and my dad was standing there with my mom right behind him.

Sammy didn't seem intimidated as he reached his hand out to shake my dad's. "Mr. Morgan?"

My dad eyed him hesitantly, then shook his hand. "Yes, that's me. And you would be?"

"I'm Sammy, Maya's friend." He smiled back at me, then turned to my mom. "And Mrs. Morgan, it's such a pleasure. You're even more beautiful than Maya said you were."

Okay, this boy was laying it on thick. Even though my mom was pretty, I had never even mentioned her to him.

My mom smiled, shaking his hand. "Why thank you, young man."

"We were just coming out here because my daughter was being quite rude leaving the house and not telling us anything about you."

Sammy nodded like he understood. "I'm sure she's just anxious because we're going to an exclusive event tonight, but I would never disrespect you or your home by just swinging through to pick up your daughter."

I rolled my eyes. But both my parents smiled proudly. Okay, so maybe Sammy knew what he was doing after all.

"Now, that's what I'm talking about," my dad said. "I didn't know you young fellas today still got that."

"Don't know about other young fellas"—Sammy grinned—"but I was raised better. A young man never pulls up and honks for a young lady."

"I think I like you." My mother laughed. "Do you want to come inside for a minute? Our maid makes some wonderful tea cakes."

That was my cue. I scurried to his side. "No, he doesn't want to come in. We need to get going."

"Maya, don't be rude," my mom said.

"Mommmmm," I protested. "Tea cakes? Seriously?"

"Maya's right. We need to get going. But, it was nice to meet you," Sammy said.

"You, too," my dad replied. "It's great to see such a well-mannered young man. Come around anytime. Maybe my daughter can learn a thing or two from you."

"Bye," I said, waving over my shoulder as I pulled Sammy toward the car.

"Really?" I said, once we were in the car.

Sammy flashed a sly grin. "I told you if you want to win, you gotta know how to play the game."

I couldn't help but smile back. Sammy had definitely played my parents well. He probably could spend the night and they'd be just fine. Okay, maybe that was a bit much, but I could tell they definitely were feeling him.

I snuggled close to him. I know it was just our second date, but I felt like I'd known him forever. "So, are you gonna tell me how you managed to get these tickets."

"I told you, you're not the only one connected," he

replied. "I just want you to have a good time. That's all you need to be worried about."

"I definitely could get used to this." I didn't know how Sammy was so well connected, and I dang sure didn't know how my cousin knew somebody like him, but whatever. I was feeling Sammy and was even willing to sit back and let someone else be the star—for at least a minute.

Chapter 11

Was it possible to fall in love in a week? Okay, I may not have been in love, but I was definitely deep in like with Sammy Martin. This guy was all that and more.

Sammy was a record producer, a behind-the-scenes guy who didn't like to flaunt his success. I didn't know how well he was doing, but obviously with the way he was balling, he was pretty successful. He'd played some of his demos for me, and he was actually pretty good on putting together sounds.

In the past week, he'd wined me and dined me. Every time he picked me up, it was a new adventure. I was very well traveled and cultured so it was hard to impress me, but Sammy was doing a pretty good job. I hadn't thought there was a lot I hadn't seen and done, but Sammy changed that.

But it wasn't just the places he took me. He was fun to be around. I could see why he and Travis were such good friends. They were both funny. Sammy had an awesome sense of humor and he was the perfect gentleman. He definitely made me feel special.

Yeah, I knew we were moving kind of fast, but when you know it's right, you just know. Like tonight. Last night, we'd gone to a private party for one of the Miami Heat players.

Tonight, we were at an opening for the Underground Railroad exhibit for the National Cultural Museum. Usually, I wasn't into any depressing slavery stuff. But I was really feeling how knowledgeable Sammy was.

"This is an original copy of *The Souls of Black Folk*," Sammy said, pointing at a huge book sitting in a display case. "I'm actually reading that now."

I frowned. "I thought you weren't in school."

"I'm not," he replied. "I need to be in somebody's college, but . . ."

"Then what are you reading that for."

That made him laugh. "To educate my mind. You don't read?"

"Yeah, magazines, and Ni-Ni Simone and Nikki Carter are some of my favorite authors, but that"—I pointed at the book—"that's like school reading."

He laughed again and shrugged. "I like fiction, but I prefer nonfiction. It helps you be a better person."

Yeah, I was gonna let him have that one. Give me my made-up stories any day. But still, something about that whole educated thing definitely impressed me. I'd never met a guy who read books like *The Souls of Black Folk* just because.

"So where to now?" I asked once we had finished looking at the exhibit. I was really feeling Sammy, but I had been saving my goodies. The guy who got this had to come majorly correct, and while Sammy was definitely a contender, he wasn't there yet.

"I'm not ready to take you home," he replied.

I flashed a sexy smile. "We can go back to your place, but I don't want to give you any ideas."

"Well, I have some asbestos issues, but we can go by my friend's place."

I raised an eyebrow. "A friend's place?"

"It's not even like that," he quickly said like he could tell

I wasn't feeling that idea. "You'll get to come to my place. I've just been staying at my friend's while they get that asbestos cleaned out."

That didn't even sound right. Asbestos?

"Naw, I need to get home. I'm working on this story I need to do some digging on." I knew my now-cold demeanor told him I wasn't happy.

He snuggled up closer to me. "Don't be like that, babe. We can go by my place if you'd like. I can show you all the work they're doing. I just don't want you to stay there."

That actually made me feel a little better. Maybe he wasn't trying to hide something after all.

"Well, hello. If it isn't Sammy Martin."

We both turned to face a pretty, brown-skinned girl with long jet-black hair. She was wearing a purple wrap dress with a slit that revealed some perfectly toned legs.

Sammy sighed, but before he could say anything, she stuck her hand out toward me. "Hi, I'm Patricia. Sammy's girlfriend."

Sammy shook his head, pushed her hand away, and said to me, "My ex-girlfriend." He pulled me close to him. "This is my girlfriend." He didn't know it, but he had just earned major cool points with me.

I could tell Patricia was struggling to keep her smile. It was icy, though. "Oh, was she your girlfriend last night?"

I couldn't believe this chick was trying to play me like that. She had the wrong one. I turned to Sammy and frowned. "You were with her last night?"

Patricia put her hands on her hips. "He sure was. Took me to dinner, then back to my place." She looked me up and down. "For grown folks stuff."

Sammy looked like he was shocked at my question, but I kept talking. "So when you claimed you went to the bathroom while we were at that VIP party last night, you actually snuck off, took her to dinner, then back to her place 'for grown folks stuff,' and were back with me in five minutes?" I asked, pretending I was horrified.

Sammy actually smiled when he realized I was being sarcastic. Patricia lost her smile.

"I guess I'm just that good," Sammy said.

I turned back to Patricia. "Or she's that bad that it only took you five minutes to handle her."

She folded her arms and wiggled her neck. I could tell Sammy was proud of the way I'd managed her.

"Glad you warned me about your psycho ex," I told Sammy, glaring at her. He hadn't, but he played along.

"What do you want, Patricia?"

"I just came to say hello. Does your little girlfriend know everything about you?"

"On that note, we're out."

She laughed. "I'm going to take that as a no," she said.

Sammy ignored her as he pulled me away. Once we were outside, I did ask him, "What is she talking about, do I know everything about you?"

"Tricia is always trying to start mess." He pulled me closer and kissed me. "But you know the most important thing about me—and that's that right now, I'm right where I want to be, with who I want to be with."

That was music to my ears.

Chapter 12

I had to give it to my cousin. He'd done good.

I watched Sammy bob his head to the sounds of the artist coming from the booth. We were inside a small studio in West Miami.

"That sounds good, man, but we need to try it again," Sammy said, leaning and speaking into the microphone. "I know you can give me better than that."

The guy in the booth frowned, and looked like he had an attitude. Personally, I thought it was a little disrespectful, but I didn't want to get all up in Sammy's business.

"So from the top, one more time," Sammy said. "And this time, act like you're a multimillion-dollar rapper."

The guy shook his head like he was irritated, but he went back to rapping while the melodic beats filled the studio.

I sat in the back and watched Sammy work his magic. I was so happy he'd let me come into the studio and watch him work. I knew my share of people, but I had never gotten up close and personal and watched music being created.

After a few more minutes, Sammy said, "All right, Jax, good job. I'm gonna jet with my girl. Y'all take it from here."

Once outside the studio, I hugged him. "Thank you for letting me get a glimpse inside your life. I'll have to have you come down to the station sometime."

"Sounds like a plan." Sammy pushed the elevator down button. "But now, you see what I do. A lot of my artists are doing the underground circuit. I have one artist who is about to sign a major deal."

"Have you written anything I've ever heard of?" I asked as we got on the elevator.

"You ever heard of 'All Gold Everything' by Trinidad James?"

I turned and looked at him. "Oh my God, who hasn't heard of that?"

Sammy smiled coyly. "Yeah, yours truly penned that."

"Are you freakin' kidding me?"

He shrugged. "Yeah, but me and Trinidad ended up falling out. He tried to get over on me, and I ended up having to take him to court. He retained the rights, but I got my money."

"I know that's right, and at the end of the day, that's all that matters. You can go write some more songs."

He took my hand and led me off the elevator. We had just stepped outside the building when a scrappy-looking guy came up to us. He looked like he had stepped straight out of a crackhead movie.

"Yo, Sam, my man, what's up?"

Sammy stopped and looked at him in horror. Sammy didn't speak as he put his arm around my waist and shuttled me off.

"Come on, man, don't be like that," the guy said, following us. "I need to holla at you."

Sammy stopped and turned to face the guy, making sure to shield me in the back of him. "Dude, I done told you about coming around, following me."

"I wasn't following you. I swear. And I need—"

"Now ain't the time," Sammy said cutting him off.

"It ain't never the time for you, now that you all big time. But I was there from the beginning, when you was just—"

Sammy stepped to him again. "I'm gonna tell you for the last time, you need to keep it movin'."

I was watching in shock. I couldn't believe he actually knew this dope fiend.

"Oh, it's like that now? It's like that? You trying to show off in front of your gal?" He eyed my Fendi purse. "Hey, how much that purse worth?"

I swallowed hard as I pulled my purse close to my chest.

Sammy pushed the guy, hard. "Man, I will beat the—"

"Okay, okay. I was just joking." It was then that I noticed his yellowing teeth. He had to be one of the most repulsive-looking men I'd ever seen. "Come on, man, just hook me up."

"I told you to forget you know me. I told you to never, ever, ever step to me again," Sammy warned.

"You . . . you the reason I'm like this!" the guy cried, pulling at Sammy's jacket.

Sammy grabbed him by the throat and pushed him up against the wall. "I told you to back off. You of all people know what I'm capable of."

The guy's legs flailed as he tried to break free.

"I'm sorry, I'm sorry," he cried.

As soon as Sammy released him, he took off running as fast as he could.

"Oh my God," I said once he was gone. "What was that about?"

Sammy watched him dart through traffic, nearly getting hit twice.

"That's my uncle," Sammy finally said.

"What?"

"Yeah." Sammy sounded so sad. "As you can see, he's kind of strung out."

We stared in the direction his uncle had disappeared. "He said you made him like that. Why does he blame you?"

Sammy shrugged. "Because he wanted me to give him the money for rehab and I wouldn't do it."

"Why not?"

"Because he wouldn't let me take him to rehab. He just wanted me to give him the money, which means he just wanted to smoke it up." Sammy shook his head pitifully.

"Dang, I'm sorry to hear that," I said.

He took a deep breath, then turned toward me, forcing a smile.

"Look, I don't want this to ruin our night," Sammy said. "I told him until he's ready to get clean, I couldn't do anything more for him. And I meant that. But let's not talk about my junkie uncle. Tonight is all about enjoying ourselves. Having a good time."

He removed a strand of hair out of my face. I thought he was going to kiss me, but instead he just smiled and said, "Let's go. I have another wonderful night planned for us."

I couldn't help but smile. All of our nights had been wonderful. I was the luckiest girl in the world. But don't get it twisted—Sammy was pretty lucky, too.

Chapter 13

Today had been one of those days I couldn't wait to end. It had been absolute chaos at work and school today, and I was just looking forward to getting home.

I pulled into our circular driveway and was shocked to see a Porsche. That car looked familiar, but I couldn't remember from where. My dad had gotten Travis a car—a 2010 Camaro, which was parked right next to the Porsche. I pulled up behind Travis's car, then made my way inside.

"Travis," I called out as I walked into the living room. "Whose car . . . ?"

I stopped in my tracks when him and Angel jumped apart.

"You have got to be kidding me," I muttered. My eyes went from him, to her, and back to him. She quickly started buttoning her shirt back up. What was this skank doing on my sofa?

"Really, Travis?" I said.

"Hey, Maya. It isn't even like that."

"What is it like, then, Travis?" My mind immediately went to Sheridan and how just minutes ago, she had been gushing about him and how he was the best thing since sliced bread. This was exactly why I hadn't wanted them to hook up. A playa never changed his spots.

"Hey, Maya," Angel said.

I didn't bother speaking to her. "Travis, can I talk to you?" I said.

"Maya . . ."

"Travis . . ."

He groaned, then turned to Angel and said, "I'll be right back."

I stomped in the kitchen and waited on him. As soon as he walked in, I started in. "Really, Travis?"

He frowned at me, acting irritated like I was the one who'd just gotten busted. "Why are you trippin'? Dang. You worse than my moms."

"Why are you sitting up in the living room getting it on with Angel?" I jabbed my hand toward the living room. "Got her in there infecting up our furniture. You know she's the biggest tramp at school."

"Me and Angel are just friends."

"I can't tell."

"Dang, stop trippin' so much." He headed back toward the door.

"What about Sheridan, Travis? Did you forget about her?"

That made him stop and he spun back toward me. "What about her?"

"I thought you guys were supposed to be together."

"We are." He actually said that with a straight face. Dog.

I pointed to the living room again. "Obviously not if you're sitting up making out with this skank."

"I told you me and Angel are just hanging out."

"Does Sheridan know?"

He glared at me, and that answered my question.

"See, this is that mess I was talking about. This is the drama I didn't want to find myself in the middle of."

"Then don't get in the middle of it," he said. "Mind your business."

I didn't back down. "When a dude gets to messing over my best friend, it is my business."

"Even if that dude is family?"

"Yeah, even if that dude is family."

We stood facing off for a few seconds. Then finally, he relaxed and said, "Maya, it's like you said—you got your life and I got mine. So just stay out of it. Me and Sheridan are just kickin' it. She knows what's up." With that, he turned and walked out of the kitchen.

Ugh, he made me sick. I stomped into the bathroom. My first thought was to call Sheridan and tell her to get her behind over here. But that would lead to more drama. Nah, I was just gonna leave it alone. For now.

Chapter 14

"So, when do I get to meet this new man?" Kennedi stretched out across my bed and examined her sandstone-painted nails. Ming, my nail technician, and her crew had just left and, as usual, had done a fabulous job on our nails and feet.

"You will. I wish you could meet him tonight, but he's out of town," I replied as I held up my fifth outfit, trying to decide what to wear to the party tonight.

It was All-Star weekend and Shaquille O'Neal was throwing a big bash. At first, I hadn't been feeling going to some old dude's party, but Sammy had sworn that Shaq threw some bomb parties, so he'd gotten me three VIP tickets because neither he nor Travis could go. Travis had gone home for the weekend and Sammy had had to go out of town with one of his artists. So, I had actually found myself getting excited about partying with my girls.

"Him and Travis are gone. Dang. I was looking forward to hanging with Travis," she said. "But I definitely wanted to meet this dream man."

She picked up my iPhone and looked at the picture I'd

taken of him at the VIP reception. It was my screen saver and looked better than anything I could've even thought about downloading.

"Girl, this boy is super fine," Kennedi said.

"Do I ever date anyone who isn't?" I laughed.

She tossed the phone back down. "I'm just trippin'. It's like I was just here a few weeks ago and you didn't even know this dude. Now, you're all in love."

Kennedi and I had been friends since we were little. Our mothers had been friends for years. But she lived in Orlando now, so we didn't get to hang as much. Still, she had been there through every guy I'd ever dated—from my first boyfriend to my last. And she didn't hesitate to let me know what she thought of someone, so I was anxious to see what she thought. Sheridan had met Sammy when the three of us and Travis had gone out to dinner the night before. Of course, she'd liked him, but right about now, she was more concerned with making sure Sammy liked her since he was Travis's boy and all. I'd never seen Sheridan act so thirsty, and it was so not a good look. I'd also told Kennedi about Travis and Angel. She told me my first loyalty was to Travis, but I definitely knew that she was biased as far as that was concerned because she didn't care for Sheridan.

"So, where did this Sammy come from?" Kennedi asked. "I mean, I know Miami is big, but anyone who is anyone, we know. So he must not be anyone." She sat up on the bed, being careful not to mess up her nails or toes.

"Oh, trust. He's someone. I'm telling you, it's like everybody knows him." Just thinking about how well connected he was had me smiling.

"Where does he go to school?"

"He's out of school."

That made Kennedi sit up some more. She loved her some older guys. "Oooh, is your mom gonna go for that?"

I shrugged as I decided on the outfit I had originally planned to wear. "It doesn't matter if my mom likes him or not, he's here to stay. But the way he'd dazzled her, she hadn't even bothered asking me about his age. She just wanted to know more details like who were "his people" and if I really liked him."

Kennedi laughed. "That sounds just like your mom. So how old is he? When did he finish school?"

"He just graduated three years ago," I said. "So he's not a whole lot older than me. He's twenty-one."

"Where is he from?"

"What is this? Twenty questions?"

"Just answer the question."

I laughed at my friend. "He's from here."

"So he is from Miami?" She shook her head. "I just don't get it. Why haven't we ever met him? He must not be in the *in*-in-crowd."

I smiled as I thought of the way Sammy worked the crowd at that VIP reception. I knew why girls swarmed around J. Love, but Sammy had guys *and* girls jocking his every move.

"Sammy's the type that makes his own crowd. Everywhere we go, someone knows him. It's wild."

"Wow," Kennedi said. "So what does he do?"

"He works as a record producer."

"Doesn't everybody." She rolled her eyes.

"No seriously, I went to his studio with him. He was straight runnin' things." I leaned in the mirror at my vanity and dabbed some lip gloss on.

"I guess if he's getting love like that, he must be on some Diddy type of ish."

I shrugged. I knew Sammy was low-key. He didn't like to talk a lot about his business. He said that the singers that he worked with didn't like him telling their business, which was probably why we hadn't heard of him.

Kennedi must've lost interest in the conversation because she said, "Anyway, what time are we heading out for the party?"

I shimmied into my skinny jeans, took one last glance in the mirror. "Perfection. So, yes, let's roll!"

Chapter 15

Membership had its privileges. I loved being not in the in-crowd, but *the* in-crowd. I bounced to the front of the line, past all of the nobodies standing out in the cold Miami air hoping that they could get inside.

Sheridan met us at the club—I half expected her to bail on us, but then, since Travis had gone home for the weekend, I guess she decided to make some time for us—or me—because she didn't really cut for Kennedi and the feeling was mutual.

The three of us strutted into the club, looking fly, as usual. I had tickets in hand so that there would be no drama about us getting in. We handed them to the girl at the counter, then made our way inside.

"This party is jumpin'," Sheridan said as she bounced to the sounds of Rick Ross filling the club.

We took in the sights and sounds. This was definitely an upscale crowd. Everyone was dressed to the nines and the ratchetness was at a minimum, thank goodness. Probably because tickets to the event were two hundred and fifty dollars.

After a few minutes, Sheridan leaned in and said, "Hey, is that your friend, Lauren?"

Both Kennedi and I turned to where Sheridan was pointing. That was Lauren. Kennedi, Lauren, and I used to be really good friends back in the day, but after Lauren's parents sent her away to boarding school, she had gotten a little too wild for our taste. Yeah, we did our own dirt, but we kept it classy. Lauren just acted like she didn't care anymore, which was obvious from the way she was dancing on the table right now, tossing her hair from side to side as she did a slow dance to the fast rap music.

Kennedi leaned in and whispered in my ear, "OMG, get your girl."

"She was your girl first," I mumbled back.

"Look, that guy has his phone up her skirt taking pictures," Sheridan exclaimed.

I shook my head in stunned disbelief. That was the kind of stuff that would come back and haunt Lauren. Not to mention she looked like a loose stripper the way she was dancing on that table.

"Come on," I said, pulling Kennedi in her direction. "This is freakin' ridiculous."

We pushed our way through the crowd, and Kennedi pushed back the guy who was taking the picture.

"Hey," he said. "I'm trying to get pictures of the freak."

Kennedi ignored him as she tugged on Lauren's skirt. "Lauren!"

I couldn't say anything. I was too shocked at the way her pupils were dancing. She looked like some kind of drugged-out groupie.

"Lauren," Kennedi repeated. "What are you doing?"

"Heeeeeyyyy," she sang.

"Are you all right?" Kennedi asked.

I wanted to tell Kennedi of course she wasn't all right. She looked a hot mess.

"Baby, I'm better than all right," Lauren said as she did a little spin on the table. Since it was a small table, of course she fell. Several people around the table cracked up laughing, but

Lauren didn't seem fazed. She stood up and tried to get back up on the table.

Kennedi grabbed her arm. "Nah, I think you're good."

Lauren snatched her hand away. "Let go of me. I got to finish getting my party on." She looked over at a girl who was passed out in a chair next to the table. "Tabitha, tell them to leave me alone."

Tabitha didn't move. Kennedi dragged Lauren in the direction of the bathroom. She stumbled as she tried to keep up.

Sheridan and I followed—I think we both were still in shock. I know I definitely couldn't believe I was caught up in this foolishness.

"You guys are party poopers," Lauren cried as Kennedi pushed her into the bathroom.

Lauren had gotten high in the past. We knew that much. But this was different. There was something about the crazed way her eyes were darting all over the place and she was sweating—hard.

"What's wrong with you?" Kennedi asked.

"Have you been smoking that stuff?" I asked.

"What stuff?" she asked, trying to play dumb.

"You know what stuff. Dope. Or crack. Or whatever it is you do," I replied.

Just then, the bathroom door opened. A plain, stringy-haired girl eased in. "Hey, I'm Piper. I'm Lauren's friend. We came here together. Is she all right?" she asked, her eyes wide with concern.

"Heeeey, Pipe!" Lauren asked. "Where you been, girl?"

"I was talking to a friend," she said. "But are you okay? I saw Tabitha passed out and them dragging you in here."

I didn't know who this Piper was, I thought I'd seen her before, but I couldn't place her. She looked drugged out herself so she couldn't have been a good influence for Lauren.

"Why everybody wanna know how I'm doing?" Lauren laughed. She smiled at Sheridan, as if she was just noticing her for the first time. "What's up, Sheridannnnn?" She leaned in toward Sheridan, who took a step back as if her "high" were contagious.

"Why you hanging around these losers?" Lauren said, her speech slurred. "You know Kennedi don't like you." Lauren turned to Kennedi. "Ain't that right, K? You said she was a backstabbing troll and you didn't know why Maya was too dumb to see it."

Sheridan glared at Kennedi, but Kennedi waved her off like now wasn't the time. "Lauren, who did you come here with?"

She pointed in Piper's direction. "With my girl, Piper. Like Peter Piper picked a piper of peppers pickled." She started giggling. Then, suddenly, she just stopped and ran her hands over her eyes like she was trying to focus. "Wh–what was I saying?"

"Lauren, have you been smoking weed again?" I asked.

Lauren started laughing like something was really funny. "Oh, this isn't your ordinary herb. This that for-real stuff." She stood up like she had a sudden burst of energy.

"What is for-real stuff?" I asked.

"This girl is on fiiiiire!" Lauren started singing, before turning and bursting out of the bathroom. She continued loudly singing, ignoring us as we called after her. We all raced out behind her, but in one swoop, she jumped up on top of the bar and continued singing her Alicia Keys song. "This girl is on fiiiiiii–re!"

Several people were looking at her crazy. I was getting pissed. I was about to tell Kennedi to leave her alone. I had an image to maintain, and chasing after my drugged-up friend wasn't part of it.

"Lauren!" Kennedi shouted over the loud music.

Suddenly Lauren stopped, leaned over, and threw up all over the bar. Several people jumped out of the way in disgust. I was about to snatch Lauren down and tell her about herself, but before I could say a word, she fell to the floor and began convulsing.

"Call 911!" the bartender shouted. I don't know much about what happened after that because my shock had just gone to a whole other level.

Chapter 16

I know Lauren is supposed to be my girl and all, and some people might say that I wasn't being a true friend. But this was the very reason that I didn't do druggies. Maya Morgan didn't need to be sitting up in some waiting room, scared out of her mind because her idiot friend wanted to get high.

"So, you're really going to bail on her?" Kennedi said.

"The paparazzi are already outside," I replied. "And the last thing I need is for me to be caught up in this mess."

"But she's our girl. We can't just leave her here." I glanced over at Piper, who was sitting in a corner nervously wringing her hands. She'd been a mess the whole ride over here. Not just because of Lauren, but apparently, their other friend, Tabitha, hadn't just been passed out. When paramedics arrived and had everyone move back, they'd noticed Tabitha wasn't breathing. She had OD'd right there in the middle of the club and no one had even noticed. Naturally, when word of her death and Lauren's episode had spread, and especially since there had been celebrities at the party, the paparazzi had come out in full force and they'd followed the ambulance right to the hospital.

Regardless, I didn't want to be anywhere near their cam-

eras when they started snapping. Sheridan had quickly re-
minded me that Lauren was my friend and she had no desire
to be sitting up in a hospital, so she'd gotten a ride home. At
first, I'd thought that was jacked up, but now, I completely
agreed.

"I just say no to drugs and anyone around me that doesn't
do that, I don't have time for. I feel bad about Lauren. I really
do. But this is whack." I grabbed my clutch and headed toward the waiting-room exit.

Kennedi looked at me like she couldn't believe me.
"Whatever."

"Call me when you're ready to go. I'll have the car service
come pick you up."

I made my way out the back entrance. When I saw the
news van from my station parked across the street, I was glad
I did.

I had just pulled off when my cell phone rang. The number came up as unknown and I almost didn't answer, but my
executive producer Tamara's phone number came up like
that. I made a mental note to tell her about that because I'd
answered one time thinking it was her and it had been some
crazed fan who had tracked down my number.

"Hello," I said, hesitantly.

"It's a dang shame that I have to disguise my number to
get you to answer."

I wanted to roll my eyes, but I found myself actually smiling for the first time since all that craziness jumped off.
"What's up, Mr. Love?"

"Oh, now, I'm Mr. Love. What happened to J?" he said.

"Yeah, I usually reserve initials for people I care about."

"Oh, so you don't care about me?"

"What do you want, J?"

"Yeah, you care about me?" He laughed.

"What do you want?" I repeated.

"You."

I'd met J. Love after an interview on my show. I don't usually mix business with pleasure, but he'd been persistent and we'd finally started hanging out. I'd really liked him, but some crazed chick who used to work for me had leaked a story about him to the *National Enquirer*. He'd blamed me, and by the time he'd discovered the truth, I had been long gone.

"Yeah, I know that, but when you had me, you didn't know what to do with me."

"A'ight. Why you always bringing up old stuff?" He chuckled. "Look, I didn't call for all that. I just wanted you to know that I'll be in town this weekend."

"Really?" Of course I knew he'd be here. His concert had been the talk of the town, but I wasn't about to let him know that.

"Yeah, really. I have a concert. I want you there."

"And I want a body like Beyoncé's. . . . Wait, I have one," I corrected myself. "But I want a lot of things that I can't get."

He laughed again. "Maya Morgan. Girl, you're something else."

"Waiting on the part where you tell me something I don't know."

"When we gon' hang out or are you still hanging with your nerd boyfriend?" he asked.

"My friend Alvin is not a nerd. He's a sweetheart. Something that you wouldn't know anything about. But it's not even like that. He's just a friend."

"Good. You need friends because I'm trying to be more than that." J. Love definitely had swag, but he wasn't about to wiggle his way back in like that. Besides, Sammy was making moves like he wanted us to be exclusive, and if that happened, J. Love could forget about ever getting me back.

"And you can try all you want, but it's not going to change a thing. So if I were you, I'd stop trying," I told him.

"Maya . . ."

"Look, J. On the real, I'm dealing with some heavy stuff

right now. I'm leaving this party and it was nothing but drama, and I'm not even in the mood."

"Oh, were you at Shaq's party? I just saw a tweet about that. Did some people really OD?"

"Yeah, and one of those somebodies was my girl, Lauren."

"Word in the Twittersphere was that that K2 was flowing freely at that party."

That made me pay attention. All this time, I'd been thinking this was Lauren's normal drugs, but there hadn't been anything normal about how she was acting tonight. And K2 would explain that.

"J, I gotta go. I'll talk to you later." I hung up before he could say a word. I quickly called Kennedi to tell her K2 had struck again and this time our friend was the latest victim.

Chapter 17

Kennedi had been so mad at me that she hadn't come back to my place last night. She'd listened as I'd told her Lauren had probably taken K2, then quickly told me she'd pass that info on to Lauren's parents before letting me have it some more for "abandoning" Lauren when she needed us most. She'd made me feel so bad that I'd gotten up first thing this morning and returned to the hospital. Now, I stood at the entrance of Lauren's room. She was awake and much calmer than she had been last night. I was so glad she was okay, but I had definitely never seen her look more afraid.

"Hey, Lauren," I said, easing into the room. "How are you doing?"

She nodded slowly as Kennedi took her hand. I didn't miss how Kennedi didn't bother saying anything to me. I was gonna let her make it, though. Kennedi was a very loyal friend, so I knew it would take her a minute to get over me leaving.

"Girl, you had us worried," I said.

"At least some of us," Kennedi mumbled, giving me a side eye.

I shot Kennedi a now-isn't-the-time look.

"I had myself worried," Lauren said, her voice weak. She was lying back against the pillow, and although her eyes didn't look as crazed as they had last night, she looked like she had been through a serious ringer.

"I don't think I've ever experienced anything like that," she said.

"Yeah, you flipped out for real," I said. "I'd never seen you like that."

She frowned, adjusted a tube that was coming out of her arm, then said, "I've never felt like that before. I just remember taking the K2, then feeling real high. I vaguely remember the whole bathroom thing, when you guys took me in, but when I went back out, my heart started beating super-fast and I couldn't breathe, then I guess I started having the seizures. I guess I was hallucinating in the ambulance ride here because I thought they were demons, coming to drag me off to hell." She shook her head. "It was unreal."

"Wow" was all I could say.

"She just woke up right before you came in," Kennedi finally said to me. "She had us all freaking out. Her parents are here. They're in the other room. Talking to police."

"This is all just so wild," Lauren said, trying to shift in the hospital bed.

I hated to hear this because I seriously had hoped that J. Love was wrong.

Lauren shrugged. "It's a new drug that Piper got." She looked away as her eyes watered up. "We were just trying to loosen up and have a little fun." She took a deep breath. "Me, Piper, and Tab . . ." Her eyes grew wide. "Oh my God." She struggled to sit up. "Where's Tabitha? I remember she passed out. Is she okay?"

Neither of us said a word as we exchanged glances.

"Where's Tabitha?" Lauren repeated as she looked back and forth between the two of us.

Kennedi squeezed her hand. "Lauren, Tabitha . . . Tabitha, she didn't make it."

That sounded like a line off some TV show, but I knew Kennedi was trying to find the right words.

Lauren sat up in her bed. "What do you mean, didn't make it?" Her eyes kept darting back and forth between Kennedi and me. "Didn't make it here, to the hospital?"

Kennedi looked to me for help.

"Lauren, Tabitha overdosed," I gently said.

Lauren fell back against the head of her bed. "Please tell me she's gonna be okay."

I shook my head. "She . . . she died in the club last night. She never even made it to the hospital."

Lauren let out a slow wail, then buried her head in her hands.

"I can't believe it. I just can't believe it," Lauren cried.

We gave her a few minutes to get her tears out. After sobbing silently, she held up her head. "It wasn't supposed to be like this."

I wanted to tell her it never was. Instead, I said, "Lauren, I don't understand why you guys—"

Kennedi held her hand up to stop me. "We're not here to preach to you about drugs," she said. "You know how we feel about them. But I heard the police say K2 is cheap, a kind of 'fake' meth. Why are you messing around with some cheap stuff?" Like our families, Lauren's was filthy rich. I couldn't see how she did regular drugs, but I dang sure didn't get why she'd be using cheap drugs.

Lauren shrugged as she slowly pulled herself up in the bed and tried to pull herself together. "My parents had been on me. Giving me these random drug tests. And this stuff doesn't show up on drug tests," she said sadly. She closed her eyes and inhaled, like she was exhausted.

"But fake means it's not real," I said. "Why would you put

some fake stuff in your body and some *cheap* fake stuff at that?"

Kennedi cut her eyes at me. I'm sorry. I wasn't going to try and sugarcoat things. That's what was wrong with these druggies. People tiptoed around them, refusing to give them the cold, hard truth. "You could've killed yourself," I added. That caused the waterworks to start back up.

"It was just for fun."

I stepped closer to her and took her hand.

"That's what I'm trying to tell you," I began. I wanted to slap her in the face with the truth, but I also knew that she was upset about Tabitha, so I didn't want to be too harsh. "This isn't normal. This stuff is killing people. I can't tell you how many stories I've heard in the past month about the dangers of K2."

She silently wept. "Where did you get the stuff?" I asked.

She shrugged. "I don't know. Piper usually gets it. But I know you can get it from any convenience store."

"You bought drugs from the 7-Eleven?" I balked.

"No, I was just saying you can get it there from a dealer," she replied, "but they do sell it at my school."

"At your boarding school?" I asked.

"They sell it at all the schools, Miami High included."

I don't know why that surprised me, but it did.

"This is bad. This is so, so bad." Lauren buried her face in her hands again. "I can't believe Tabitha is gone."

"Yeah, and it could've been you," I said matter-of-factly.

"Lauren, you know we love you, but you've gotta stop messing with this stuff. All of it," Kennedi said. I guess Kennedi figured it was time out for sugarcoating as well.

I wanted to know more about where she (or Piper) was getting the drugs. I was about to ask her some more questions when the door to her hospital room opened.

"Ladies, I'm going to have to ask you to step out," the

nurse said, entering the room. She lifted a plastic bottle hooked on the edge of the bed and measured it.

"What's that?" I asked.

"That's a catheter. That's where she urinates," the nurse said, and I couldn't help but cringe. Now, she couldn't even pee without assistance? If I did do drugs, that alone would be enough to make me stop.

"We'll be waiting outside," Kennedi said, pulling me toward the door.

Before we reached the door, Lauren's parents walked in.

"Hi, girls," her father said.

"Hello, Mr. and Mrs. Lewis," I said.

They both managed a weak smile before her mother said, "Girls, we really appreciate you all being here for Lauren, but we're going to have to ask you to step out," her mother said.

"We were just going to wait outside," Kennedi said.

"It's probably better if you go on and go home," Mr. Lewis said. The tone of his voice made me wonder if he thought we had something to do with Lauren taking drugs.

Her mother followed us out. "I'm sorry to have to do this to you guys, but we just got some devastating news and we have to figure out how to break it to Lauren."

"What's wrong?" Kennedi asked, panic spreading across her face.

"Apparently, Lauren had a loss of oxygen, which resulted in some spinal damage."

"What does that mean?"

"It means"—she took a deep breath—"Lauren may not be able to walk again."

"What?"

Her mother dabbed at her eyes.

"From doing drugs?" Kennedi asked.

Mrs. Lewis shook her head as she unraveled the tattered tissue in her hand. I reached over, grabbed the Kleenex box off the nurse's stand, and handed her a fresh tissue. She took it, blew her nose, and continued. "I've been so scared that something like this would happen, but Lauren always thought it was no big deal." She glanced back at Lauren's room. "This is obviously a very big deal." Mrs. Lewis turned to me and squeezed my hand. "I see you've been covering this on your show. I wish you could find out who's behind this and help put a stop to it. Tabitha's mother is heartbroken. She's lost her only child. And we're just thankful that . . . well, we're hoping that not being able to walk will be the worst of Lauren's problems."

I just kept shaking my head. This was all just so unbelievable.

Mrs. Lewis hugged us both. "You girls go on home. We'll keep you posted."

By this point, Kennedi and I were both teary-eyed as we watched her walk back to Lauren's room. Finally, Kennedi said, "My mom is on her way up here. She's just as upset about Lauren and she wanted to see Lauren's parents. I know what Mrs. Lewis said, but I'm just gonna stay up here and wait on my mom."

"Are you sure you gonna be okay?"

Kennedi nodded, as she wiped away her tears. "Why would she do this, Maya? Why would Lauren risk everything just to get high?"

"I don't know. I guess this stuff is pretty powerful." I didn't have the answer because I just didn't understand it myself.

"Mrs. Lewis is right." Kennedi's voice turned serious as she stared at me. "You gotta do something."

I frowned. What the heck was she talking about? "Me? What am I supposed to do?"

"I don't know. Find out who's bringing the drugs in Miami. Expose them."

"You know that's not what I do." I know I'd been covering the stories of celebrities hit by the K2 craze, but that was where the buck stopped. I wasn't some investigative reporter. And I wasn't trying to be.

"Maya, you know I don't try to tell you how to do your job, but this stuff is for real. The regular news stations are covering this K2 story, but our friends aren't listening to them. They'll listen to you! They'll take you serious and maybe even help you bust this ring. You've got to do something before another person we know has their lives messed up."

I was trying to figure out who had died and made me Captain Save-A-Druggie.

"You have a voice, Maya. Use it."

I looked at my friend. She wasn't usually this serious. About anything. But I guess this was definitely a serious matter.

Chapter 18

I'd been thinking about what Kennedi said all night. She was right. Something had to be done. And right now, I was the voice to get it done. But did I really want to get in that deep? I'd sent Sheridan a text saying I wanted to talk to her at lunch. I was going to get her opinion on what I should do. And while I was at it, I decided I was going to tell her about Travis and Angel as well, family or not. If it were me, I'd want to know. With everything going on with Lauren, I was just starting to feel like life was too short to be wasting time mad at friends. I was just going to tell her what was really going on with Travis and Angela and let the chips fall where they may.

I caught up with Sheridan before she went into the cafeteria for lunch. I'd seen Travis walk off toward the gym before I got there. He was probably going to play basketball during lunch. Good. I didn't need him around while I tried to tell her everything.

"Hey, Sheridan," I said as I approached her.

"Hey," she said dryly.

I frowned. "What's your problem?"

She rolled her eyes like she was exasperated with me. Finally, she took my arm and pulled me to the side. "Maya, you know you're my girl, but you are really tripping. I don't know why you are so dead set against me and Travis being together, but you need to get over it. We're going to be together and there's nothing you can do about it."

First of all, where was this coming from? Secondly, I know she was not coming at me like that. I looked at Sheridan and had to struggle to keep from going off. But I decided to give her a pass due to her lovesickness, so I took a deep breath and tried to continue.

"Oooo-kay. I'm not sure what that's about, but I wanted to tell you—"

"No!" she yelled, cutting me off. "You don't need to tell me anything about my man."

I bucked my eyes in shock. "Excuse me?"

She sighed as she shook her head. "Just let it go. Travis has made it very clear that he wants to be with me and you will stop at nothing to break us up. So, go somewhere with that garbage you're trying to bring me. Travis already told me."

"He did?" I asked, raising an eyebrow. I couldn't believe he'd told her about Angel and she was still taking up for him.

"Yes. And I think it's foul."

"Then, why are you acting like I'm the one who did something wrong?" I asked, getting an attitude.

"Because you're doing too much, trying to make something out of nothing."

"Wait a minute. Are we even talking about the same thing?"

She folded her arms defiantly. "Yeah, the fact that you want to take something innocent and use it as a reason to try and break me and Travis up."

"Oh, wow. Is that what he told you?"

She folded her arms and said with an attitude, "Yeah, he told me that he and Angel were studying and you came in there going off about how you were going to tell me. Well, you don't have to tell me. He did."

I couldn't help but smirk. "He did, did he? He told you all about Angel, huh? Everything? And you believe him?"

"I trust my boo."

I couldn't help but laugh at that. I didn't know when my best friend had become so dumb. "Really, Sheridan? He's my cousin. I know him better than you."

"Really, I'm beginning to think you don't."

It was my turn to take a woosah moment because I was clean about to go off. "All right, Sheridan, I'm gonna let you make it. Let's just end this conversation before you make me tell you about yourself."

"You don't need to tell me anything. Worry about your own man and leave mine alone."

I stared at her in disbelief and finally just said to myself, *Walk away*. I told her, "Whatever. You go ahead and live it up with Travis. Do you, boo."

I flicked her off as I spun and stomped away. I'd lost my appetite and had only one mission in mind—to find my cousin. I headed in the direction that I had seen him go. I couldn't believe it when I spotted Travis outside the gym, standing there flirting with Angel. I stomped over, grabbed his arm and pushed him against the wall.

"What the—"

I jabbed my finger in his face. "Look here, I know you're family and all, but don't make me go hood on you and stomp the mess out you. Maybe that's what I need to do anyway so that you can understand that you're not about to play me!"

He looked flustered. Angel backed up as well. "Maya, what in the world are you talking about?" Travis said.

"I'm talking about this whole game you're playing with Sheridan."

He gently pushed me away from him. "Chill out, cuz. I told you, it ain't even like that."

"Don't tell me to chill out! How are you gonna tell Sheridan that lie that I'm trying to create drama by breaking you two up."

He turned his lips up at me. "Are you or aren't you?"

"I'm not trying to break anybody up. No, I didn't want you guys hooking up, but if you wanna get with that slut bucket, then it's on you!" I pointed at Angel. She just rolled her eyes but didn't respond.

"Well, I just wanted to prepare her in case you decided to try and tell her. I don't need you getting her all worked up when it's not even like that."

I leaned in again. "Your girlfriend may be stupid, but I'm not." I threw my hands up in disgust. "But you know what. You and Sheridan do what you have to do. Dog her out for all I care."

I turned to leave, but Travis grabbed my arm, stopping me. "Come on, Maya, can we have a truce? I wasn't trying to throw you under the bus. I just don't want to hurt Sheridan and I didn't know what you were going to do."

"So, you just lie to her?"

He sighed. "I'm sorry, okay? I don't like fighting with you."

"Whatever."

"I'm just saying, you have your love life, I have mine. I'm not getting all up in your business with Sammy, so give me some of that same respect. There are a bunch of questions I could be asking you about him, but I stay out your business."

"First of all, you're the one who fixed me up with him. But whatever. I'm so sick of you and your stupid girlfriend."

I was so irritated, I couldn't do anything but shake my head. "So, you're right. Do what you want to do." I looked over at Angel and ran my eyes up and down her skanky be-hind. Angel was nicknamed knob at school because, as the jocks joked, everybody got a turn. I used to think that was the corniest line I'd ever heard, but it fit her perfectly. The sad part was she was pretty and rich, so she didn't need to be a tramp, but she was and now she was tramping with my cousin. "Or shall I say, do whomever you'd like. Just make sure you remember, nasty dogs carry fleas." I didn't give either of them time to respond. I just turned and stormed off.

Chapter 19

When the WSVV receptionist told me Alvin was standing out front waiting to see me, I almost didn't come. But I had my own man, so I needed to get over my issues with Alvin and go talk to him.

We spoke, but I have to admit it was dry and I could tell his feelings were hurt.

"So you're really mad about Marisol?" he asked, once I'd stepped close to the lobby door, and away from the receptionist, to talk to him.

"I'm not mad," I said. Maybe I wasn't mad, but I definitely wasn't happy, which was why I had been ignoring his calls.

"You're not mad, but I can't get a callback. I can't get you to pick up when I call. You think I don't know you're sending me straight to voice mail?" he said. "What I don't understand is why."

Me either, I wanted to tell him. I shrugged. "I don't know what to tell you except I'm not trippin' over you and your girlfriend."

"Marisol is not my girlfriend. She's just someone I was hanging out with."

"Umph."

"Look, Maya. You know I would much rather be hanging out with you, but I don't fit your image. So, you won't give me a chance—yet."

That made me smile. "Yet?"

"That's right. Yet." To be such a nerd, Alvin was definitely cocky. "Because I'm going to get you. Some way, somehow, I'm going to get you."

"My, aren't we the confident one?"

"No. I'm just keeping it real. I get that you don't want me yet. But I figured it out. It's because you don't know me."

"I do know you."

"Nah, you don't know me like that. But that's gonna change." Then Alvin leaned in and kissed me on the cheek. "Marisol is my 'in the meantime.' You're my destiny. Have a good day."

Then, with that, Alvin left and left me standing there with a "what just happened?" look on my face.

I don't know how long I was standing there in the lobby just staring at the front door after Alvin walked out through it, but the receptionist's voice snapped me out of my daze. "Maya!"

I jumped and turned to her, wondering if she had been calling me a minute. I shook my head. I couldn't believe Alvin was getting in my head like that.

"Oh, sorry. What's up, Sybil?"

"You have a call on line one," she said.

I frowned because Sybil knew I usually didn't like to take calls directly. I got all kinds of crackpots trying to contact me, and most of the time, it wasn't any information I could use.

"Who is it?" I asked.

"That's just it," Sybil replied. "The caller won't say. But she said it's about the K2 craze. She said she has some info you may be interested in."

I definitely snapped out of my daze then. "Give me a minute to get to my office, and then put her through."

She buzzed me back, and I raced to my office and picked up the phone. "This is Maya."

"Maya Morgan?"

"Yes? How may I help you?"

"Ummm, well, I see you've been doing stories on celebrities that are hooked on K2. I have some information that might interest you," the caller said.

I sat down at my desk and immediately grabbed a pen and paper. "Okay. Go ahead."

"Well, I'm not going to tell you who it is, but she's pretty big," the caller continued. "But she's started taking K2 and I've already seen the damage it's causing. She's not going to be happy till it kills her. Because of who she is, she's getting her drugs straight from the top."

My heart was actually racing. "And who would be at the top?"

"I can't tell you his name," she said.

A lot of good that's going to do me, I thought as I threw my pen down.

"But if you find one of his suppliers, they might lead you to him. You'll be stunned at who's at the top."

That piqued my interest again. "Usually, it's some high-level drug dealer."

"Usually, but in this case, it's a former A-list actor."

Now, she had my full attention. "What? What actor would throw away his career fooling with drugs?"

"One who can make more money selling drugs," she said matter-of-factly. "One who is getting older and knows his days are limited."

I wondered why this caller was giving me the story and not someplace like *Dateline* or Oprah. I thought about it, and decided this sounded seriously dangerous. Telling someone's business was one thing. Exposing something that could get someone killed was another.

"Who is this person?" I asked.

"I told you I can't tell you his name."

"What am I supposed to do with this information, then?"

"Get to his suppliers, his workhorses, and they'll lead you to the man next to the man. I watch you all the time. Matter of fact, you're the only thing I watch on TV. This story will make you even larger than you already are. I promise, look into it. It'll be worth it in the end."

She hung up the phone and left me sitting there trying to process everything she had just said. I didn't know about this. This sounded like a whole lot more than I was bargaining for. But if she was right, and a huge celebrity was behind this, I could use my voice to make a difference *and* boost my ratings? Oh, that sounded like a perfect combination!

Chapter 20

The caller's words were still weighing on my mind. I hadn't even been able to concentrate in class today because I was thinking about what she'd said. If she turned out to be right, that could be major. I'm talking *Today Show* and *Good Morning America*—Oprah might even feature me on her *Oprah Presents* show. But I didn't mess around in that underbelly world. It didn't take a rocket scientist to figure out that those folks could be dangerous, and the last thing I needed was to be caught up in some danger.

But if I played my cards right, kept the cops on speed dial, and just did what I do—report the story—it shouldn't be a problem. After all, reporters exposed stuff all the time.

But where would I start?

"Miss Morgan?"

I jumped as Mrs. Williams slammed her hand on my desk. "Is my class interrupting your thoughts?"

"No, ma'am. I'm sorry."

She pointed to the chalkboard. "So then, can you answer the question?"

I stared at the board, and I swear, it was a bunch of jumble with historic dates and arrows pointing everywhere.

"Uh, I'm sorry, can you repeat the question?"

"No, I cannot," she said, glaring at me. "I need to see you after class." Then, she walked away to go harass another student.

I sighed. I so did not need this right now. I waited and let all my classmates file out; then I walked up to her desk.

"Yes, ma'am, you wanted to see me?"

She looked up at me over her wire-rimmed glasses. "Miss Morgan, I have been more than lenient with you, have I not?" Mrs. Williams said.

"Yes, ma'am."

"You turn in substandard work, you miss crucial tests, don't turn in homework, and you half come to my class. Now, I understand that you're a 'superstar.' " She used her fingers to make quotation marks. I wanted to ask her what the heck was that supposed to mean. But I didn't say a word. "But let me be very clear," she continued, "even superstars flunk the twelfth grade."

My eyebrows raised in horror. Would she really flunk me?

"And if you think that I won't flunk the great Maya Morgan, you are sadly mistaken."

I wanted to protest, speak up in my defense, but I knew Mrs. Williams and just stood there and took her verbal lashing.

"Have you studied at all for next week's exam?"

Really? Next week, as in a whole seven days away? Of course I said, "Yes, ma'am, I have."

"This test is do-or-die for you. I would suggest you devote as much time to your coursework as you do to exposing other people's secrets. Get it together, Miss Morgan."

I nodded. "Yes, ma'am."

"Good-bye, Miss Morgan."

"Good-bye," I said before I turned and walked out of the room.

I wanted to tell her what I really thought about her and

her stupid test. But she was right. She had been lenient with me, so my best bet was just to keep my mouth closed.

Sheridan greeted me just as I walked out her classroom.

"Hey, are you in trouble?"

I shrugged. Sheridan had been trying to act all cool with me and as much as I tried to stay mad at her, she was my BFF, so it was hard. "No more than usual. Mrs. Williams was just getting on me."

"What did she want?"

"To complain. She says I don't pay attention in class, I'm too focused on my job, yada, yada."

"She is so lame. She wishes she had your job. What does she make, seventy-five thousand dollars a year?"

I cringed. "Isn't that poverty level?"

"I bet she's on food stamps."

We busted out laughing as we walked toward the parking lot. I was glad I'd made up in my mind to leave her and Travis alone. I missed my girl.

"Hey, there's that girl that was with Lauren at the club," Sheridan said, pointing to some girl leaning against a railing, smoking a cigarette.

"Who?" I peered, trying to see who she was talking about.

"You know, Piper's friend."

"Who the heck is Piper?"

"You know, from that night at the club when Lauren passed out. The one who went to the hospital with us," Sheridan said.

My mind started racing. I hadn't been able to get in touch with Lauren to try and get next to Piper, but this girl could connect me with her.

"Come on," I said. "Let's go talk to her."

Sheridan paused. She had a look like she knew she was about to make me mad. "I can't. I'm about to go meet—"

I held my hand up to cut her off. "Whatever. I'll talk to you later."

I darted over to the girl. "Hey!"

The girl stopped smoking and looked around, trying to be sure that I was talking to her.

"Jodi, isn't it?" I said, stopping in front of her.

"Yeah," she said, eyeing me skeptically.

"When I saw you at Shaq's party the other night, I thought I'd seen you before," I said. "I didn't know you went to Miami High."

She continued looking at me strangely. "Yep, all four years."

"So, what's going on?" I tried to appear casual.

Her eyes darted around again, and she seemed to be waiting on some surprise to pop out. "Ummm, nothing." She was speaking really slowly, as if she was expecting me to do something.

I know she was wondering why I, of all people, was coming to talk to her because I'd never said a word to her in our entire time at Miami High.

"Where you going?" I asked.

"Umm, home."

"Well, look, I wanted to ask you a question. You know the other night at the club when you were with Tabitha, Lauren, and Piper?"

"Yes?"

"Well, I know you guys were kind of indulging . . ."

Now, she looked a little nervous. "I don't know what you're talking about," she said, sounding guilty as all get-out.

"Chill, I'm not the cops. I'm not trying to get anyone in trouble. I just need a little something to take the edge off myself. Me and Lauren go way back, so I know everything. I just wanted to get a little something for myself." I hated having this girl thinking I was into drugs, but I didn't know how she'd react to me saying, "Oh, I'm trying to do an exposé on druggies and the people who supply them with drugs."

Jodi just stared blankly at me.

I continued. "So, just between you and me, where can I find some K2? I don't like dealing with middlemen because you know I have a whole lot of money and I need to keep things on the low-low."

"Again," she said, slowly, "I have no idea what you're talking about."

"Look, Lauren is one of my best friends, so I know what's up. You don't believe me, ask her. She knows I'm legit, I just need a little something to keep the edge off." I didn't know how drug addicts acted when they were trying to get high, but I rubbed my arm for effect (I'd seen that on TV).

She studied me for a minute, tossed her cigarette, and said, "Wow, I didn't know you were into that."

I forced a smile. "That's the way it should be. Nobody should know your business, right?"

Jodi finally relaxed. "K2 will definitely do that, but it'll also have you trippin'."

"Can you hook me up? You know, tell me where you get yours from?"

She shook her head. "I don't know where we get it from. Piper is the one that gets it."

"So you don't know where Piper gets it from?" I asked.

"Nope. She just shows up with it and I don't ask questions." That was so freakin' ludicrous to me. How are you going to just take random drugs without even trying to find out where they came from?

"Well, can I get Piper's number?" I asked.

She looked at me like I was crazy.

"Okay, can you text Piper?" I suggested when I saw how she was looking.

She didn't move.

"Come on. Just ask her to call me, Lauren's friend that was at the hospital with her."

Jodi sighed, then took the phone out and tapped. "A'ight, I texted her."

"Thanks a lot." I turned to leave.

"Hey, Maya," she said, stopping me. "I don't like to tell people what to do, but be careful with that stuff. It ain't no joke. I'm sticking to the basic stuff after what happened to Tabitha. That K2, that's a feeling I don't ever need to experience again."

I nodded. "Thanks a lot." She just didn't know I knew how dangerous it was. That was why I was determined to bring attention to the drug and, hopefully, shut the K2 ring down.

Chapter 21

When I pulled up to my house, I was surprised to see Sammy's car there. He and Travis were sitting outside looking like they were in an intense conversation.

I pulled up behind Sammy's car in our circular driveway and got out. When they saw me, they immediately stopped talking.

"Hey, guys. What's going on?" I asked as I approached them.

Travis's brow was furrowed and he looked stressed out.

"Hey, babe," Sammy said, a huge smile across his face as he leaned in and kissed me.

Travis grumbled something so I turned to him and said, "What's wrong with you?"

He kind of shook his head like he was shaking off whatever was bothering him.

"Nothing. I'm straight," he replied.

"I think Sheridan is lookin' for you. Weren't you guys supposed to be meeting up?"

He nodded. "Yeah, I saw she called. But I, um, I got a little tied up."

"My, are we to the point of ignoring her calls already?" I smirked.

"Maya, don't start." He turned to Sammy and gave him some dap. "Man, I'll holla at you later." He frowned at me as he walked back in the house.

"What's his problem?" I asked.

"He got into an argument with his mom so he's just buggin'. He'll be a'ight." Sammy pulled me closer. "How was your day?"

"It's fine. Working on a story."

"You're always working on a story. What is it?"

I started to tell him, then decided I was tired of talking about the whole K2 situation.

"Nothing." I motioned toward the house. "So what you gettin' in today? You wanna come inside or go somewhere?" I asked.

"I'd love to, babe," he said. "But I gotta get out of here. I have to meet someone at the studio."

"Oooh, can I come?"

"Nah, it's a closed session." He kissed me again. "But I gotta get out of here for now."

I said good-bye, then made my way inside.

I looked around for Travis, and when I didn't see him, I figured he must be in his room. I headed up the stairs and stopped just outside his door. His door was cracked and he was pacing back and forth. Whatever it was he'd gotten into about with Aunt Bev definitely had him stressing.

I was just about to say something when my cell phone rang. I looked down and didn't recognize the number. I answered anyway.

"Hello," I said, stepping away from Travis's door so that he wouldn't hear me.

Silence.

"Hello," I repeated.

"Yeah. It's Piper. You wanted me to call?"

My heart started pacing. "Hey, Piper. This is Maya, Lauren's friend."

"I know who you are," she said hesitantly.

"So did Jodi tell you what I wanted?"

"Yeah, but I'm not buying it."

I knew if I wanted Piper's help, I'd have to be honest, so I said, "Okay, I'm not really trying to buy any drugs."

"Tell me something I don't know. So why are you trying to track me down?" Piper said. "Lauren is always talking about how squeaky clean you are so I can't imagine what you want with me."

Me, squeaky clean? Well, I guess compared to them, I was a Girl Scout.

"First, let me say I'm sorry to hear about Tabitha."

It sounded like she swallowed a lump in her throat. "Thanks. She was my best friend."

"Secondly, Lauren asked for my help. She wants me to help bust the K2 ring, or at least bring some attention to it." That wasn't exactly the truth. It was actually Lauren's mother, but Lauren was locked away at rehab so it wasn't like she could confirm anything. "I want to find out where the drugs are coming from."

She was quiet before saying, "I don't know if you want to do that."

"I do, and I need your help."

More silence, before she said, "What you want me to do?"

"I want you to help me figure out who's behind it. I want you to take me to meet the person your dealer gets his drugs from."

That actually made her laugh. "Girl, you've been watching too much TV. I don't know who that is." She let out a long sigh. "But I can take you to Antoine, my new dealer. I'm not messing around with my old guy anymore after that mess he sold us at the party."

"So your new guy, he sells the K2?"

"Yeah. I've only met him twice, but he's cool and I really don't want to get him in any trouble. . . ."

"I understand that. And I'm not trying to get him in any trouble. But we've got to do something," I warned. "How many more Tabithas have to die?"

"I guess," she slowly said. I couldn't be sure, but it sounded like she was crying.

"Thank you so much for helping me."

She was quiet for a minute before saying, "If it can save one other person, then it's worth it."

"That's all I'm trying to do."

Piper blew a long breath. "Maya, I feel like I have to tell you, this is serious stuff. You're playing with fire."

"You just lead me to your dealer and I'll take it from there," I said.

"Okay. I'm telling you, be careful what you ask for, but I'll do it. I don't even want to know what you plan to do once you meet him. I'll just make the introduction, then you're on your own."

That was all I needed. "Okay. When can we do it?" I needed to let Tamara know what was going on.

"Well, there's a party this weekend. It's one of those private things for those of us who, umm, who indulge. I'm supposed to be meeting him. We can hook up there."

"Sounds like a plan. And Piper, you're doing the right thing."

Her voice was sad as she replied, "Too bad it's too little too late." She hung up the phone without saying good-bye.

Chapter 22

I stood outside the door to Tamara's office. She and Dexter were inside. I knew once I told them about this story, there would be no turning back so I had to psych myself up again. Did I really want to get in this deep?

Yes, like Kennedi said, I had to use my voice.

"Knock, knock," I said, lightly tapping on her door. Tamara was sitting at her desk; Dexter was in front. "Can I come in?"

"Hey, Maya, come on in." She motioned to the seat in front of her desk next to Dexter.

"There's my superstar," Dexter said, a huge smile across his face.

"We were just going over the numbers," Tamara said. "Girl, this show is through the roof. It's doing better than any of us ever expected, especially in our target market, the eighteen-to-twenty-five demo."

I didn't understand any of that TV jargon she was talking about. "If you're trying to say that everyone is watching my show, tell me something that I don't know."

"Kelley told me you have a whole list of appearance requests coming in left and right," Tamara said.

"I know. I just asked that she be a little more selective in what she has me doing because I don't do malls anymore."

"Yeah, you're bigger than that," Tamara said.

"Way bigger," Dexter added. "Is the exclusive with Savannah still on?"

"Yep, just confirmed. As soon as she gets out of rehab we'll set up the interview. She promised not to talk to anyone else."

Both Dexter and Tamara grinned widely.

"So, what can I do for you?" Tamara asked. "Or did you just stop through to say hello?"

I took a deep breath. This was it. No turning back. "Actually, no. You know we've been covering a lot of celebrities hit by the K2?" I began.

Both of them sat up like they were waiting for some blockbuster revelation.

"Yes?" Tamara said.

"Please tell me you have exclusive details on someone major?" Dexter said, his eyes dancing excitedly.

I side-eyed him. Was he really getting excited and worked up about someone getting hooked on drugs?

"No. No A-listers. But I think I may have a line to one of the dealers. He's the man next to the man."

"I'm not understanding," Tamara said.

"Apparently, the K2 is being funneled into the country through Miami. And I know someone who can get me next to one of the dealers. I was thinking if we could get the exchange on tape, we could do a whole exposé on it."

Dexter frowned. "Yeah, that sounds like a job for *20/20* or *Dateline*."

I knew I had to tread carefully because Dexter cared about ratings. He couldn't care less about being some voice or stopping people from dying. I had to present it in a way that he could relate to. "No, here's the thing, this thing is taking out celebrities left and right, right?"

Both of them nodded. Tamara studied me like she was trying to see where the story was going.

"Well, we've been covering that, but my source also tells me the man at the top is a former A-lister."

Dexter looked like he was about to pass out. "Oh my God. Who?" he asked.

"Not sure yet, but that's what I'm trying to find out," I replied. "There's a party this weekend that I'm going to and I was hoping to get an undercover camera or something to get some stuff on tape."

Tamara shook her head. "Ummm, I don't know. . . ."

"So, all I'm saying is imagine how many people would be using and crediting our video if we have teen celebrities and rich kids and teens in general getting high on the drugs. We could have undercover video of them in action," I continued. "And you'd have video of the dealer as well."

Even though he'd gotten excited, I could see Dexter still wasn't completely sold. "I'm still not seeing what that has to do with rumor and gossip."

"Everything isn't in the moment," I said. "It's about the big picture as well. It will bring even more people to *Rumor Central*. It will get our name out there more and who knows, maybe we can help bust up the drug ring."

Tamara shook his head. "Nah, I'm still not feeling it."

Dexter held up a hand. "Wait. I think I see where you're going with this. And where are you getting this undercover video?"

"Like I said, my connection is taking me to some exclusive party. It's supposed to be some of everyone there. And it's my understanding they get pretty wild."

I knew I needed to reel them both in. "Imagine if the video caught someone like Orlando Franks? I hear he runs in those circles."

Orlando was a Miami-based actor who was among Hollywood's elite teen stars. At the mention of Orlando's name, Dexter's eyes perked up. "Orlando's going to be there?"

I thought about telling him the truth—that I really had no idea—but I figured I'd get further if Dexter thought there was even the slightest chance of getting an A-list actor like Orlando on tape buying drugs.

"Well, I heard through the grapevine that he would," I said just to get Dexter on board.

"Wow, I guess you're right," he said.

"If we can get video of all these celebrities getting high and get the dealer that's supplying them with this K2 on tape, then all the major networks will air our video and say our name, which will put our brand out there even more," I said.

Dexter started nodding. "Okay, okay, I'm with this."

Tamara, however, wasn't smiling. "I don't know, Maya. I get what you're saying, but I'm not feeling right about placing you in harm's way."

I sighed heavily. "Look, Tamara, I'm going to the party, regardless. So the only question for you all to decide is if you're going to put an undercover camera on me."

She shook her head with finality. "The more I think about it, the more this sounds too dangerous."

Dexter had a look on his face like a good story was slipping through his hands.

"Well, it's not like we're telling her to go," he said. "We told her not to go. But since she's going anyway, we might as well fit her with a camera."

See, this was why I wanted Dexter on my side.

Tamara hesitated. "How do you know this isn't dangerous?"

"It's not. It's just a party. It's not like the drug lord is going to be there. It's just her dealer and some people who are into heavy drugs and partying. And I'm going to see what other information I can gather."

"Okay, what about Mann?" Tamara said, asking about the

man who worked part-time as my bodyguard. "That's the only way I'll feel comfortable, if Mann goes with you."

"Tamara, what will that look like, me walking up in this place with a six-foot-four, three-hundred-pound man with me? Nobody is going to talk to me," I protested.

"Well, we could have him—"

"No. I repeat, I'm going to the party by myself. You can put a camera on me or not. That's it," I said sternly.

Tamara sighed heavily. "Okay, I hope you know what you're doing. We can get the tech team to get you a lapel camera. It's small and can just be worn like a pin on your shirt. But honestly, we're going to have to have you sign a waiver that this is something you're doing against our advice because the station can't be held liable if something happens."

"That's no problem," I said. I had to do this, with or without them. I was just glad that they were now on board.

Chapter 23

I was nervous as all get out. I wasn't used to this serious under-cover work. The more I thought about it, the more I liked the celebrity gossip side. *This is as real as it gets,* I thought as I looked at the crowd of people gathered outside the spacious West Miami house. There were whites, blacks, Hispanics, Asians, even a few Indians. It looked like the United Nations up in here and they all had one thing in common—they were all high as kites.

"You ready?" Piper asked me.

I nodded. I must've looked unsure because she added, "Now's the time to change your mind. After this, there's no turning back."

"I'm sure," I said. "I think," I mumbled under my breath. I made sure my lapel pin was on and recording everything.

"I told you, be careful what you ask for," Piper said as she led the way inside.

Some guy approached us just as we made our way into the crowded living room. "Yo, Pipe." He waved a small bag of blue pills. "I got that good stuff."

"Nah, I'm straight," Piper said, although I could've sworn her voice cracked as if that was the hardest thing she'd ever had to say.

He turned to me. "What about you, cutie pie?"

Cutie pie? I hadn't been called that since the third grade. "Yeah, no thanks. I'm good," I said.

"Y'all some busters." He opened the bag and popped a pill in his mouth. I watched him dance away to the thumping house music that filled the room. Somehow I had the feeling that this wasn't his first pill of the day.

Throughout the living room, I spotted people doing all kinds of drugs. Some were smoking. Some were sniffing. It was all just too much. And those who weren't getting high were getting plastered with some kind of grape-looking concoction. Piper had taken a cup from someone who was passing the drink out. I'd told them no thanks. They probably had drugs in the drinks.

"Where is your dealer?" I finally asked Piper.

"Chill. I told you Antoine was going to meet me here, so he'll be here. Don't try to holla at him, though. We don't mix business with pleasure," Piper warned with a smile.

"*As if.* Trust, I will not be trying to holla at a drug dealer."

"Hmph. When you see him, I bet this is one exception you'll make because he is fine with a capital F."

I truly doubted that, but I didn't say anything as Piper grabbed my arm and dragged me into the other room.

"Come on," she said. "You could at least try and enjoy yourself while you're here."

The whole environment was so not my thing. It seemed like everyone was drunk or high or trying to get drunk or high. Then, there were people kissing and making out as if they were in the privacy of their own room. It was like one big freak fest.

I made sure that I got video of everything. So far, I hadn't recognized anyone. Dexter would be sad to hear that, but oh well, that really wasn't my mission anyway.

Finally, after about fifteen minutes, I asked, "What time is he going to be here?" I asked. I was hoping this thing didn't end up being a bust.

"He should be here soon," Piper said, glancing at her watch as she sipped some strange-looking drink—something else I'd passed on. No telling what these people were putting in these drinks. After a few minutes, she looked around, then said, "Oh, there he is." She grabbed my arm again and pulled me through the crowd.

"Hey, handsome," Piper said, wiggling up to a guy who had his back to us.

"What's up, girl?" he said, turning around.

My mouth fell open as I yelled, "Travis?"

He immediately lost his smile, and his eyes widened in horror. "Maya?"

"You two know each other?" Piper said, confused.

"Oh my God. What are you doing here?" I asked. I felt like I was in the middle of a bad dream.

"I could ask you the same thing," he replied.

Piper looked back and forth between the two of us. "This is the guy that I was telling you about."

"*This* is your drug dealer?" I asked.

She draped her arm through his. "Antoine prefers not to be called a drug dealer." She giggled.

"I don't know what else you'd call it, *Antoine*," I said, looking at my cousin in disbelief.

"Let me holla at you," Travis said, grabbing my arm and pushing me out the side door before I could protest.

"What do you think you're doing?" he asked once we were on the back deck.

"No, the question is, what are you doing?" I said, snatching my arm away. "You're dealing drugs, Travis? Really?"

Travis massaged the back of his neck. "Come on, cuz. Don't do this to me."

"Answer the question," I demanded.

"I'm just dabbling in a *little something*."

"Peddling drugs to teens is not a little something."

He huffed, running his hands over his head. He seemed scared, nervous, and in disbelief. I guess he never expected to be busted.

"So this is the job you have? Selling drugs?" I demanded to know.

He spun on me. "You know, you're trying to turn this all around on me. What are you doing out here trying to buy drugs?"

"I'm working!" I exclaimed. "Trying to track down a drug dealer."

"For what?"

"Because that's what I do." I inhaled and shook my head as I went inside my shirt and turned my hidden camera off. "I have a hidden camera and everything to record the jerk who's selling people drugs!"

Travis looked absolutely horrified. "Maya, what are you doing?"

"I told you, busting a drug ring."

He shook his head and started pacing back and forth. "You don't know what you're getting into."

"Yes, I do. I just didn't know my cousin was the drug dealer I was investigating."

Before I could say anything else, gunfire rang out. I screamed as I dove to the ground. People started frantically running out. Travis managed to grab my arm and pull me as he took off running.

"Where did you park?" he yelled as we neared the street.

My heart was racing. "I didn't. I rode with Piper. My car is parked at the mall."

"Come on." This time he didn't wait for me to keep up. He didn't have to. I was right on his heels, trying to get away and desperately wondering how in the world I'd ever gotten caught up in some madness like this.

Chapter 24

The ride home had been a quiet one. I was so flustered I told him just take me to our house. I'd get my car tomorrow. In addition to being scared out of my mind, I had an attitude and so did Travis, although I definitely couldn't understand why he would be tripping with me. He was the drug dealer, not me.

"Stop looking at me like that," he finally said as he slowly turned his car onto our street. We'd driven the whole way home in silence. I was so mad at him I didn't know what to do. I had been staring at him for the past fifteen minutes, and he'd just kept acting like he didn't see me, until now.

"Looking at you like what? Like, 'wow, my cousin is really a drug dealer'?"

"I keep trying to tell you, I'm not a drug dealer." He gripped the steering wheel like he was trying to keep his anger in check.

"Do you or do you not supply drugs to druggies?" I asked.

He sighed like he wished he could make me disappear.

I didn't care. When I'd started digging into this story,

never in a million years would I have thought my own cousin was behind it.

"I just got a little side hustle going on, that's all," Travis said.

"A side hustle? For what? If it's for Aunt Bev, you know we'll help."

He slammed the steering wheel with his palm, pulled into our driveway, took a deep breath, then turned to me. "You don't know what I need, Maya, so stop trying to judge me."

"Oh, please," I said. "Matter of fact, does Aunt Bev know what you doin'? Is that why she wanted you to leave Brooklyn? Were you dealing drugs in Brooklyn?"

He pointed a warning finger in my direction. "Like I said, shut your trap because you don't know nothin' about nothin'."

I shifted, turning in my seat so I could get a better look at him. "I know that even if you were slangin' up in New York, you don't need to be doing it now. I know that much!"

"Don't act all holy. You were there to buy drugs so it's not like you're some kind of angel."

"No," I corrected him, "I was there to try and dig up dirt on the jerk who was dealing drugs that are killing people, so imagine my surprise when I find out the dealer is my own cousin." I shook my head in disgust.

"Why are you investigating this?" he said, exasperated. "I thought you were some kind of celebrity reporter. This ain't even the kind of stuff you do."

"Usually, I am, but your drugs are hitting celebrities and now it's personal, too. My friend Lauren could've died. Did you give her those drugs?" I stared at him, because if he had, then that meant he was responsible for Tabitha's death. "Well, did you?" I repeated, waiting on him to answer.

He shook his head. "No. I couldn't meet Piper, so she told me she was going to call another guy." He sighed. "It's just a cheap high."

"It ain't 'just' anything," I said. "And I hope you're not trying to justify this mess."

He looked flustered himself. "Maya, just drop it and mind your business, okay?"

"Digging up dirt is my business."

He put his hand on my arm. "Maya, this ain't no simple celebrity gossip. You don't want to get caught up in this mess."

His voice was so serious it scared me. But still, I said, "You mean like you're caught up?"

"Look, just listen to what I'm saying." He squeezed my arm. "This is serious. Leave it alone."

"You're not the boss of me!" I said, jerking my arm away. "Maybe my dad can help you come to your senses."

He glared at me, his eyes blazing. "So now you a snitch?"

I turned up my lips at him. "Oh, please with that ghetto foolishness. Number one, I snitch for a living. Number two, I don't live by some kind of jacked-up street code." I wasn't about to tell my dad on Travis—he'd kill him if he knew he was associated with any kind of drugs. But if thinking that I might tell could make Travis come to his senses, then let him think it.

"Maya . . ."

"No, Travis." I stopped him. "This stuff is serious. People are dying."

Travis ran his hands over his face

"Why are you doing this?" I continued. "You don't have to. I don't care what things were like back in New York. They're different here. You don't have to do it. Just walk away."

"It's not that easy, Maya."

Silence filled the car.

"So, I guess you're gonna tell Unc?" he asked after a few minutes.

I sat in the passenger's seat with my lips poked out. I should march right inside and tell my dad everything. But even though Travis made me sick right about now, I really liked my cousin. If my dad found out he was dealing drugs, he'd have Travis on the first thing smoking back to New York.

"I'm not gonna say anything." I sighed. "But you gotta get outta that game."

He looked so relieved. "After tonight, I am. This could've ended real bad."

"Ya think?" I said, pointing to my lapel pin.

"Okay, okay. It was just temporary anyway. Just don't tell Uncle Myles."

I nodded. As long as he kept his word and got out of the game, I would keep my word and keep his secret.

Chapter 25

Travis and I stared at one another as he approached me in the hallway. I don't think I'd ever had a time when my cousin made me as mad as I was right about now.

I'd heard him on the phone last night, talking about making "one last delivery." I'd busted in and charged him up. He'd been mad, talking about I was spying on him. Well, I was, but still . . .

"Okay, what's going on with you and your cousin?" Sheridan asked as she noticed our stare off.

"Hey, babe," Sheridan said, leaning in and giving Travis a hug. He half-hugged her as he gave me the evil eye, which Sheridan immediately caught.

She stepped back and looked between the two of us. "What's up?"

"Why don't you ask your boyfriend?" I said, folding my arms across my chest. I know he was wondering if I had told Sheridan. I'd wanted to, but I just couldn't. I didn't want anyone, not even my BFF, knowing my relative was a drug dealer.

Travis just kept glaring at me. "Are you two arguing again?" Sheridan asked. When neither of us replied, she shook her head like she was somebody's mama and I was the child who wouldn't listen. "Maya, get over it, okay? I told you, you're just going to have to accept that me and Travis are going to be together."

I don't know what Travis was doing to her, but maybe he'd been slipping her some of those drugs he was selling because, clearly, she had lost her mind. "Oh, you're together, huh?"

"Yes." She leaned in and hugged Travis tighter.

"Y'all boyfriend and girlfriend, right?"

"You know that," Sheridan replied confidently. Travis was standing there looking like a stupid bump on a log.

"But does your boyfriend know that?" I half smirked as I turned to Travis. "Do you know that, Travis?"

"Maya, don't start with me."

"What does that mean, does your boyfriend know that?" Sheridan asked.

Travis pulled her closer. "It doesn't mean anything, babe. She's trippin' as usual."

Sheridan sighed, then looked at me all serious. "Why are you guys always fighting? You're supposed to be family."

"Whatever, Sheridan." I opened my locker, then threw my book inside and slammed the door. "Ask your boyfriend what's wrong." I rolled my eyes as I walked off.

I had just made it out to my car when I bumped into my former *Miami Divas* co-stars, Evian and Shay. Our relationship had been rocky since all that drama, but I wasn't in the mood, so I told myself to just be nice and keep it moving.

"Hey, Evian. Hey, Shay," I said as I approached them.

They said hello back, even though I could tell they still had attitudes. But that's okay. I knew after all the drama that went down, we'd never be the same.

I was about to keep it moving when Evian said, "Hey, I saw you and your new guy at that new seafood restaurant the other night."

I stopped and turned back to her. "Sammy? Yeah, that's my boo."

"Sammy?" Shay said, frowning like she was surprised. "What's his last name?"

"Martin, why?"

I swear I saw a smirk on her face, but she didn't say a word. If this girl told me she had been with Sammy, I thought I was going to die. "You know him?" I asked her.

She smiled, but then slowly said, "Nah, I don't."

I could tell Shay was lying. Even Evian looked at her strangely.

"Come on, let's go," Shay said, pulling Evian away. "See you around," she told me as Evian gave me a confused wave good-bye.

Unh-unh. Something wasn't right. As soon as I got in my car, I pulled out my phone and called Sammy.

"Hey, beautiful," he said, answering on the first ring.

"Hey."

"What's wrong? Why are you sounding like that?"

I debated coming right out and asking about Shay. I normally wasn't the jealous, insecure type—I didn't need to be. But there was something about Shay that got under my skin.

"Hey, babe. Did you hear me? What's wrong?" Sammy repeated.

Just as I was about to say something, images of Sammy talking about the way his ex was trippin' that night at the museum flashed through my mind. No, I wasn't insecure and I wasn't about to let Shay make me doubt my man. Or myself.

"Naw, nothing's wrong. I'm just tired," I flashed.

"Well, you can't get too tired, because I'll be through to swoop you up. What time will you be done taping tonight?"

"I don't have a taping tonight. So, I'll be good after school. What are we doing?"

"Just hanging out. We can go to my boy's crib and chill."

"Why can't we hang out at your place?" I'd been trying to get over to Sammy's, but something always came up. I was beginning to wonder if he was like Alvin and lived with his mom, or worse, some woman. "You got someone living there that you don't want me to know about?"

"Come on, Maya. You know me better than that. I told you that they're treating my place for asbestos. I know you don't want to mess up that pretty little face by getting sick."

I definitely didn't want or need that. But he'd been running that asbestos line on me since we met and it was truly getting played.

He must have known I was getting an attitude because he said, "Don't be like that, babe. There will be plenty of time for you to come over."

Since he was already trying to pacify me, I decided to go ahead and ask about Shay. "Well, look, there is something on my mind. I just bumped into one of my classmates and your name came up."

"My name? Why would my name be coming up with a bunch of high-schoolers?"

"My point exactly," I said. "One of my classmates saw us out the other night. But when she said your name, the other girl had some kind of reaction that I couldn't read."

"What kind of reaction? And what girl is this?"

"Her name is Shay Turner. She's Jalen Turner's daughter."

"Jalen, the basketball player?"

"Yeah." I held my breath. "Please don't tell me you've ever gotten with her."

He laughed. "Nah, boo. I told you. I don't usually do young chicks. You are the one and only."

I didn't know whether to be flattered or insulted. I knew I was mature for my age, but I didn't like being referred to as a "young chick."

"I promise you, Maya, I've never gotten with anyone from Miami High so relax. Nothing for you to be stressed out about."

I don't know why, but I believed him. Maybe because I knew Shay and while we'd buried our major differences, she wouldn't hesitate to let me know if she had gotten with my man.

"Okay, it's cool," I finally said. "I was just asking."

"Maya, one of the things you will never, ever have to worry about is some other girl stepping to you talkin' about she's doing anything with me. You got that?"

"Got it," I said, a smile finally creeping up on my face.

"Now what time will I get to see you? After the day I've had, I need to just chill."

"Well, call me Dr. Freeze 'cuz helping you chill is my specialty."

"You are so corny."

"But you know you love it."

"That I do." I laughed.

"And I love you, too," he said.

That made me stop. A brief silence filled the line. Then I said, "I love you, too, Sammy Martin. I love you, too."

Chapter 26

I fluffed my hair in my handheld mirror one last time, rubbed my lips together to make sure my lipstick was evenly smoothed out, then handed the mirror to my hairstylist, before turning my attention back to the camera.

"Stand by," my director, Manny, said. "Cue music, and five, four, three . . ." He pointed at me to go. The theme music wound down and I immediately went into my zone.

"Hello and welcome to *Rumor Central*, where we dish the dirt on the celebrities you love. Lovelies, grab your shovels because I'm about to give you the scoop! We all know the K2 craze is spreading like wildfire. Now you know I keep it real. I don't usually get *this* real, but, folks, K2 is as real as it gets. This gossip diva has no idea what it is about this drug that makes celebrities—and people in general—willing to risk everything, but that's exactly what it's doing. Another A-lister has bit the dust—the K2 dust, that is." I threw my hands up like I was confused. "Do you bite K2? Smoke it? Is it a pill?" I leaned in toward the camera in a dramatic fashion. "I wouldn't know because I don't get down like that. But do you want to know who does know?"

A mug shot of Atlanta rapper Krush popped up on the

screen. "You all may know superstar rapper Krush. Well, he's gotten a hold of that Kush—K2 to be exact. And, it messed him up so bad that he crashed his Ferrari into a tree. Why can't police stop it? This drug is out of control and it seems like the problem is going to get a whole lot worse before it gets better. Your girl is all over this story to see what celebrity K2 will bring down next." I waited for Krush's before and after photos to pop up again.

"So remember, if you want the scoop, you know we're doing the digging. Until next time, holla at your girl."

The music came up in our spacious, trendy studio as we went to commercial. I removed my earpiece as I shook my head at the picture of Krush. He looked worse than Savannah. Why these people would do this to themselves was beyond me.

"Got another one. Country music star Lee Bryant just got admitted to the hospital. They said it's K2," Dexter called out from the producers pod.

I shook my head as I exited the studio. They'd have to deal with that one. I'd had enough. I wanted to go back to call girls, secret babies, and cheating mates.

I gathered my stuff and got of there before they decided they wanted me to go back on the air or something. This was all just too draining.

Twenty minutes later, I was pulling into my driveway, ready to get inside and just relax. But before I could get inside, Travis met me at the door.

"Maya, what are you doing?" he said, frantically.

"Ummm, trying to come home." I pushed around him and went inside.

"No, I'm talking about your story." He closed the door and followed me inside.

I tossed my bag on the floor. "What about it?"

"I saw the story you just did."

"Okay, and?" I was tired and not in the mood. If he had something to say, he just needed to say it.

"Maya, you just need to leave this alone," he pleaded.

I folded my arms. "Why? You don't want me to expose your business?"

"Maya, I told you I'm out of the game."

"And I told you, I don't believe you, especially after that phone conversation."

He balled his fists like he was getting angry. I raised my eyebrows to let him know I wasn't moved.

"Maya, these are some ruthless people you're trying to expose. Some real ruthless people."

"Okay, who are they?" I said, looking him dead in the eye.

"Maya . . ."

"No. Who got you in this game? Where do you get your drugs from? I'm gonna keep at it. Maybe if I bring all this attention to this story and bring down the kingpin, you'll come to your senses."

Travis shook his head "What makes you think you can bring down somebody the entire Miami PD can't touch?"

I shrugged. That was a good question, but Miami PD lacked one key quality—they weren't divalicious like me.

"Maya, just drop it okay? You said if I got out of the game, you'd leave it alone."

"You're not out and after you lied to me, I don't believe you're going to get out, so I'm just gonna keep at it, until you walk away."

He blew a frustrated breath.

"Okay, Maya. But I'm warning you. This is a very dangerous game you're playing."

I waved him off. I wasn't stupid. I planned on being careful, but this thing had gotten out of control. I had a voice on *Rumor Central*, and I was ready to really use it!

Chapter 27

I needed to learn to just stay out of Sheridan and Travis's relationship because this back-and-forth, arguing and then making up with Sheridan, was getting old. Even still, when she called and acted like nothing was wrong, I just blew it off and told her to come over since Kennedi was in town.

Honestly, I really loved having my two BFFs together, even though they really didn't care for one another. They were my two best friends in the whole world and couldn't stand each other. So I was forced to do stuff with them one at a time.

Although Kennedi hadn't really cut for Sheridan for the longest time, she really couldn't stand her after Bryce and I broke up a few months ago because he'd let Sheridan fill his ear with a bunch of gossip. Sheridan had been mad at me about the way the whole *Rumor Central* thing had gone down and had tried to pay me back by kicking it with him. Kennedi had thought what she'd done was super foul and that I shouldn't forgive her, but me and Sheridan go way back and I'm not going to let some boy come between us. Even a boy as fine as Bryce.

They both were mad because I refused to say which one

was the better BFF. I wished that I could say all three of us would be close. They both were my girls and I loved when we could all hang out without all the drama. Today was one of those rare days.

"I'm glad you invited me over," Sheridan told me. "It's been a while since we just hung out."

I wanted to ask her whose fault was that, but I just bit my tongue.

"I'm surprised Maya has got time for me today," Kennedi joked as *Real Housewives of Atlanta* played in the background. We'd been watching a marathon of the show. I loved the ratchetness of it all, although my favorite was *Real Housewives of Beverly Hills*. Those chicks had real money. Those Atlanta housewives had make-believe money.

"What are you talking about?" I replied.

Kennedi turned her lips up at me. "You're talking about Sheridan, but you're always up under Sammy."

"Whatever." I laughed, tossing a pillow at her. That erupted into a full-blown pillow fight.

We finally settled down, and Sheridan said, "How's Lauren doing?"

Kennedi plopped back on the bed. "She's better, but her parents have her on serious lockdown. She's in rehab right now, but when they take her out they're going to home-school her."

"Rehab is so nineties," Sheridan said, shaking her head.

"Whatever, she needs to get that under control," Kennedi said.

"Do you think she's going to?" I asked.

Kennedi nodded. "Yeah, I think Tabitha's death really scared her. It's like it was a wake-up call because she didn't protest at all when her parents told her.

"So you had any more drama out of Patricia?" Kennedi asked.

I shook my head. "As a matter of fact, Sammy showed me

a text from her yesterday. He wanted to make sure I saw it so she didn't play any games."

"How do you know he's not really getting with her?" Kennedi asked pointedly.

I shrugged. "I don't. But I trust him. Get you a man and you'll understand." I snapped my fingers at her.

I could do that because I knew Kennedi wasn't fazed about not having a man. She liked being footloose and fancy free as she called it.

"Yeah, bring your A-game like me and you'll snag the perfect guy and you won't have to worry about him stepping out," Sheridan added.

I could tell Sheridan was joking, but I couldn't tell if Kennedi knew she was joking. I held my breath as she cut her eyes at Sheridan. For a number of reasons. Number one, I didn't want Kennedi snapping. But number two, I'd told Kennedi about Angel and I prayed she didn't use that opportunity to throw it up in Sheridan's face.

"Oh, yeah, I forgot, you all in love with Travis," Kennedi said.

Sheridan did a slow twirl. "And Travis is in love with me."

"Please don't get me started," I said, rolling my eyes.

"Maya just hatin' because we're about to be family."

I hated seeing Sheridan's nose wide open, but I stayed out of it.

"So what would you do if you found out Travis was cheating on you?" Kennedi asked all innocently. I gave Kennedi the evil eye, but she ignored me. "I mean, how would you handle that?"

"Well, first of all, that wouldn't happen," Sheridan said.

I knew Sheridan had really only been with Logan, who had treated her like a queen. They'd only broken up because he had gone overseas to college in London. But really? She couldn't be that naïve.

"You can never say never," Kennedi said. "On any guy."

"To only be eighteen, you sure are bitter," Sheridan told her. "Haven't you ever had a soul mate?"

"I'm not bitter," Kennedi replied. "I'm just realistic. And soul mate? Wasn't Logan your soul mate? Weren't you guys destined to be together forever? How long was your forever? Two years?"

Sheridan cut her eyes at me.

"Unh-unh, don't pin that one on me," I said. When Sheridan had been with Logan that had been all she'd ever talked about.

But Sheridan shrugged. "You can say whatever you want. Nothing is going to change my mind that Travis is the one."

"Okay, if you say so."

"I say so."

I was no longer smiling because now was the perfect time for me to come clean, tell her all about Angel. She'd cut me off the last time I'd tried to tell her, but I needed to just tell her everything right now. But for some reason, I stayed silent. I knew that meant that if and when Sheridan ever found out about Travis and Angel—and found out that I knew—things were most definitely going to get ugly.

Chapter 28

My cousin had come barreling into my world, creating nothing but drama. I'd suspected that he was still dealing, but now I was sure. I'd overheard him on the phone again this morning. Just like before, he was talking about making his "last delivery." I thought about going in and busting him, but what good would it do? He was just going to lie about it. Now, I'd been thinking about my next move—telling my dad—so much that I couldn't even enjoy my date.

I sat across the table from Sammy, toying with my peach salmon.

"You're not hungry?" he asked. I know he was wondering what was going on because I hadn't been real talkative since we'd sat down to eat.

"Nah, I'm just a little stressed out. Got a lot on my mind." I set the fork down.

"Like what?"

I sat silent for a minute; then Sammy took my hand.

"Maya, I want to be here for you," he said. "Let me. You know, when Travis first hooked me up with you, I'm gonna be honest, it was just something to do. But I'm really feelin' you, girl. So let me be there for you. Tell me what's going on. You can talk to me."

I took a deep breath and said, "Travis and I had a fight."

"So what else is new?" Sammy relaxed, as if he was glad that was all that was wrong. If only he knew. "Y'all always fighting, giving each other a hard time, But you know you're gonna make up."

"I know, but this is different." I paused, wondering just how much I should tell Sammy. Travis was his boy, but he couldn't have known what my cousin was doing. Sammy was one of the good guys so I didn't know if he'd even understand. I also didn't want to rat out my cousin, but I needed to talk with someone about it. "We've been arguing for a couple of weeks now and I'm really worried about him. Did Travis mention anything about what was going on to you?"

Sammy leaned back in his chair. "Why don't you tell me?" The look on his face told me that Travis had told him something, but he wasn't going to sell Travis out either, so I decided to go ahead.

I leaned in and lowered my voice. "I don't know how much you know, but Travis is caught up in that K2 drug ring. I found out he was actually selling it."

Sammy slowly nodded, but didn't say anything.

"What do you think about that?" I asked, hoping he would be just as upset as me.

He shrugged. "I think it ain't my business."

That wasn't the answer I had been hoping for, but I just said, "Well, it's mine because I think he's in a lot of danger."

"I'm gonna be honest with you," Sammy said. "Travis is my boy, but you're my girl and I think you need to stay out of that."

"Well, it's too late now. I'm working on a story for my station. That's how I found out about Travis. I set up an undercover sting."

"I think you need to go back to the regular stuff you used to do because this game is real and you don't want to get caught up in it."

Okay, Sammy was really making me mad. He was supposed to take my side. "And I don't want him caught up in it. But now, you're sounding like Travis," I said.

He put his hands over mine. "Don't get upset with me. I just think you should leave it alone."

"Whatever, Sammy," I said.

"Come on, Maya, don't be mad. Let me be honest. I know what he's doing. I'm trying to get him to leave it alone. Travis is messing around with some people that don't play, and from what I understand, he isn't in that deep so he can get out."

"So you know about it?" I looked at him in shock.

"I just found out a couple of days ago."

"I want him to leave it alone."

"I get that. But he's eighteen—he's grown. And you don't need to be getting caught up in that mess."

"I'm thinking about telling my dad," I admitted.

"I wouldn't do that," Sammy said, shaking his head. "I think it would mess up you and Travis's relationship for good. And then your dad would just send him back to New York and probably tighten his rope on you."

"I don't want him to be sent back, but I don't want him to get caught up in any trouble."

"I'll talk to him," Sammy said.

That sounded like a good idea because I knew Travis wouldn't listen to anything I had to say.

"Now, can we just enjoy the rest of the night?"

I nodded. But until my cousin was out of the game—I mean, truly out of the game—I didn't know how I'd enjoy anything at all.

Chapter 29

I'd made up in my mind that I wouldn't tell Sheridan about Angel, but I would tell her about the drugs. If Travis really was feeling her like he claimed, maybe she could help me put pressure on him to leave the drugs alone.

Sheridan and I had just left our last class and were walking out to the parking lot after school. We both stopped dead in our tracks at the sight of Travis in his car.

"Is that . . . ?" Sheridan said, leaning in and peering in the direction of his car.

I inhaled and immediately wished we had taken the back way out. Angel was sitting in the front seat of Travis's car and they were slobbing each other down.

"Sheridan," I said. But it was too late, she was already stomping toward his car. I'm sure she didn't know who the girl was, but I had no doubt it was Angel, especially when I saw that horrendous, bright yellow shirt that she had been wearing earlier. Besides, I'd known this day would come. I'd hoped it wouldn't, but my gut had known that it would.

"Sheridan," I said again, racing after her. She stopped in front of Travis's car, watching them as if she wanted a picture burned in her memory. Then, she pounded the hood. Travis and Angel jumped apart. He immediately began freaking out as he opened the door and scrambled to get out.

"Sheridan!"

"I can't believe you!" she screamed. "And you, tramp!" Sheridan hightailed over to the passenger side as if she was planning to pull Angel out of the car by her hair and give her a beat down right there in the school parking lot. But Angel wasn't stupid. She locked that door so fast it was almost funny.

But there was nothing funny about the way Sheridan was acting right now. Divas didn't get down like that.

When she saw Angel wasn't about to unlock the door, she came back over to Travis and began swinging on him.

"I can't believe you! And then you have the nerve to do this in the middle of the school parking lot."

"Come on, Sheridan. It's not even like that." He struggled to grab her hands to keep her from hitting him.

She snatched her hands away. "Get away from me!" She pounded the hood again. "Get out of the car, trick!"

Angel was no fool. She stayed in that locked car as Sheridan went crazy.

I finally managed to pull Sheridan back. "Sheridan, come on now. You are not some hood rat. You need to handle this diva style," I whispered. I motioned with my eyes to the small crowd that had started gathering to watch the show.

That must have sent a jolt through her because she took a breath and wiped her tears.

"Why you bring her over here?" Travis said, turning his anger onto me. "You said you weren't going to say anything."

I could've slapped Travis myself. Sheridan looked at him, then back at me.

"You knew about this?" she asked in disbelief.

"Sheridan, look . . ." I was exasperated with this whole situation. This was the drama I didn't want to be caught up in. I took a step toward her. "Come on, let's go talk."

"You knew about this?" she mumbled again in disbelief.

I sighed and turned to my cousin. "No, idiot. I didn't tell her. You're the one sitting out here making out with that tramp in the middle of the parking lot."

"How could you do this to me?" Sheridan said. The jacked-up part was that she was looking at me.

"I tried to tell you not to mess with him," I said defensively. "That's my fam and I love him but you're the one who went behind my back and got with him."

"So you're gonna pay me back by not telling me that he's cheating?" she asked. "You're supposed to be my best friend."

By now, the small crowd had moved in closer. See, this is that mess I was talking about.

"Sheridan, I'm sorry," Travis said. "It's just she—"

"Don't you talk to me," she said, her voice a lot more calm as she spun in his direction.

I stepped up. "Sheridan, you deserve better. . . ."

"And you don't talk to me either." She turned and ran off. I wanted to go after her, but I was pissed myself. How did I end up being the bad guy in this? I told both of them not to mess around.

"Dang it," Travis mumbled. He seemed really upset.

"I hope it was worth it," I snapped. "Jerk."

He glanced back and the car, where Angel was sitting in the front seat, trembling.

"Nah, it wasn't worth it," Travis softly said, like he was mad at himself. "I don't even like shorty like that. It's just she . . ."

I looked at Angel buttoning up her shirt over her gigantic boobs. Yeah, I knew exactly how she had lured my cousin. But I wasn't about to let him off that easy.

"You're trifling, Travis." I jabbed my finger in his face. "I don't even know who you are anymore. You're selling drugs. Trying to play my friends. You make me sick."

Just then, we heard a loud scream. I looked to see where it was coming from. It was just a few feet away. It was the stringy-haired girl from my calculus class. She had fallen to the ground in tears. A group of people had gathered around her and were trying to console her as she screamed and cried.

"Nooooo, not Lin," she cried.

I guess it was the reporter in me because I flicked Travis off and made my way over to the commotion.

"What's going on?" I asked one of my classmates.

"You know Lin Vo, the valedictorian?"

"Yeah, I have calculus with him. What about him?" I asked.

"He died today. You know he had overdosed and been in the hospital."

"From dope, right?" someone standing next to us asked.

"From that K2," the guy said just as Travis approached. I looked at him to see if he had heard. Judging from the look of horror on his face, he had definitely heard.

Chapter 30

"What's wrong with you? Are you still mad at me?" Travis asked. I'd ignored him all evening. I was so mad at him and I was mad at Sheridan for being mad at me, so I didn't have anything to say to either one of them.

I stared at Travis but didn't say a word.

"Come on, Maya. Don't be like that."

I put my magazine down and stared him directly in the eye. Travis was always playing around, but this was serious and I needed him to know it. "First you playing with my girl's heart and now, Lin died from those drugs you're selling."

Travis lost his smile. "I didn't have anything to do with that. I don't sell at school."

"Okay, so he didn't get it from you. But who knows, maybe the next person that does get it from you will end up just like him. I just don't understand how you can get caught up in this. You haven't been here that long—how could you be hooked up with a drug dealer so fast?"

Travis let out a long sigh. "Look, you don't know my world."

"Even if that *was* your world, it isn't anymore," I protested. I was about to put anger aside and try to reason with him. I was done. If I couldn't get through to him, my next step was to go to my dad. "You have a good life here." I motioned around the house. "You have everything you ever wanted."

His eyebrows narrowed together and his nostrils flared. "No, Maya. *You* have got a good life. This isn't my home. Yeah, Uncle Myles and Aunt Liza are trying to make me feel welcome, but at the end of the day, if I slip up, I'm gone."

"Then don't slip up," I said matter-of-factly.

"Do you mess up? Yeah," he said, not waiting for me to answer. "And if you do, nothing's gonna happen. If I do, I'm outta here. And it's just a matter of time before I'm not good enough. So, I'm trying to get a better life for me and my mom."

"By selling drugs?"

"By any means necessary!"

I didn't know how to get through to my cousin, but I had to get him to see he needed to get out of the drug game. "You know, my dad is not gonna turn his back on you."

"If my own dad would turn his back on me . . ." Travis caught himself, like he was trying not to get angry. "I'm not counting on anyone but me and my mom."

"Travis, that's crazy."

"You would think so," he snapped. "You lead a privileged life, Maya. But the rest of us, we gotta do what we can to survive."

"But you're family. Mom and Dad treat you like you are. Anything you want, they give it to you."

"Until they don't. My mom won't ask your dad for help. There's a reason for that."

I shrugged. As much money as my father had, he could pay for whatever Aunt Bev needed, so I didn't understand why she didn't want to ask.

"Why won't Aunt Bev let him help her?"

"Because Uncle Myles made her feel like a failure and she

refused to beg. She wanted to make it on her own. That's what I'm trying to do."

"But you're trying to make it by selling drugs." I sighed heavily. It was like nothing I was saying was getting through to him. "How'd you even get involved in that game?"

He blew a frustrated breath. "Look, I had a connect that used to come up to New York. I hooked up with him down here. It wasn't supposed to be permanent. It was just to get a little stash."

"How much do you need, Travis? I have some money—I will give it to you."

He actually looked insulted. "I'm not some kind of leech. I work for mines."

"Selling drugs isn't work."

Travis threw up his hand like he was tired of this conversation. "It's not even that serious. I'm out of the game so why we even having this conversation?"

"So you're really out of the game now?" I asked, trying to decide if I was going to tell him about the latest conversation I had overheard.

"Yes."

"Whatever, Travis." I couldn't believe he was just going to keep lying to me. Well, now I knew what I had to do. "I'm done." I stood and walked toward the door. "I tried to give you a chance. Now you left me with no choice." With that, I headed down the hallway toward my father's office.

Chapter 31

I stood outside my dad's office, wrestling with my decision. I was seriously scared for Travis because this drug was no joke and according to sources in the newsroom, police were really about to start cracking down on it, so the last thing I wanted was my cousin going to jail. Not only because he wasn't the jail type, but how would that look for me?

"Hey, sweet pea, how are you?" my dad said once he noticed me standing in the doorway.

"Hey, Dad. You got a minute?" I asked.

He motioned for me to come in. "I've got just a minute." He shuffled through some papers on his desk. "I have an important meeting I'm getting ready for."

I sighed. He always had an important meeting. I thought about going to talk to my mom but quickly nixed that. She would hear the word "drugs" and have Travis on the first plane back to New York.

I sat down in the tall wingback chair in front of my dad's desk. "Can I ask you, why'd you bring Travis here?"

My father stopped for a minute, then looked up at me. "Why? I thought you'd enjoy having your cousin around. You guys used to be so close when you were little."

"Nah, he's cool. I like having him here. I was just wondering why you decided to bring him here."

My dad finally gave me his undivided attention like he was trying to figure out where this conversation was going. "Well, my sister is just having a hard time."

"Travis said Aunt Bev is sick. Is that true?"

My dad nodded. "Yeah, Bev's not doing too well and the stress of Travis getting in and out of trouble is only making things worse. He was running with the wrong crowd and the judge said this was his last chance. So, this is kind of the last shot. It would probably kill my sister if it didn't work out here," my dad sadly said. "So, I really appreciate you working with me on this. I can imagine that it can't be easy for you since you're used to being an only child. I'm very proud of you, Maya."

Oh great, I thought. How was I supposed to tell him about Travis now?

"So, why'd you want to talk to me about Travis? Is something wrong?"

I paused. I couldn't do it, especially after what he'd just said. "That's actually not what I wanted to talk to you about." I thought for a moment. How would I get out of this now? "I'm working on this story for the station," I continued. "What would you do if you found out someone you knew was selling drugs?"

"*Drugs?* I would call the police and turn them in myself." Somehow, I had known that would be my dad's answer. He'd always made it clear that the two things he would not tolerate were stealing and drugs.

"What if it was a relative? You would turn in your own flesh and blood?" I asked.

"Absolutely." He narrowed his eyes at me. "Morgans don't mess around with drugs."

I forced a smile. "Dad. It's for a story, I told you. You know

I'm not about to mess up all of this." I motioned up and down my body.

My dad narrowed his gaze. "Is it Travis? Is he doing drugs?" I could see the panic on his face, so I quickly said, "No, Dad. I told you it's just for a story. This lady turned in her son and I just couldn't see how she could do that. That's all."

Relief immediately passed over my dad's face.

"Okay. I'm just making sure," he said, relaxing for a bit. "But no, anyone who sells drugs is a blemish on the community and deserves to be put in jail." I wondered if his answer would be different if he knew his nephew was selling one of the biggest drugs on the market.

"Okay, I was just wondering. I'm going to let you get back to work." I stood and made my way back out into the living room. Travis was standing near the front door like he wanted to be ready in case he had to make a quick getaway. I swear, I'd never seen him look so scared.

He watched me slowly walk toward him. We stared at each other until he finally said, "You feel better now that you have cleared your conscience and told Unc about me?"

I didn't reply.

He actually looked like he was trying not to cry. "I guess I need to go pack before Uncle Myles comes and throws me out."

"Nah, you don't need to pack," I coldly said. "Your little secret is safe. For now." I stepped closer. "Your secret may be safe, but are you?"

I let those words simmer as I turned and walked away.

Chapter 32

My eyes absolutely had to be deceiving me. There was no way my BFF was sitting in my living room with my cousin. In the past week, he'd become more relaxed when he saw I was holding true to my word and not telling my parents anything.

I stood in the doorway and just looked back and forth between the two of them. Sheridan's eyes were puffy like she'd been crying, and Travis was holding her hand. As soon as she spotted me, she jerked her hand away.

"Really?" I said.

"What's up?" Travis said. "How was work?"

"Work was work." I walked in and dropped my stuff on the coffee table. "What's going on?"

"I just invited Sheridan to come over so we can talk," Travis said.

"And she told you what you could do with your invitation, right?" I knew that was a dumb question since she was sitting right here. Sheridan still hadn't looked up at me. I was really mad. Here she was ignoring my calls for the past couple of days, but she'd made up with him?

"So . . . she forgave me," Travis said, smiling as he took

Sheridan's hand again. "What I did was dumb. She's the one I want and she doesn't ever have to worry about something like that happening again. She knows that. Right, Sheridan?"

This fool actually nodded.

Now I was sure that BFF had completely lost her mind.

"Everyone makes mistakes," she mumbled in my direction.

"Who are you, and what have you done with my best friend?" I exclaimed. I knew Sheridan liked having a boyfriend. But my girl was gorgeous. She could have any guy she wanted and she was going to take Travis back just like that?

"Maya, just leave it alone," she said.

I threw my hands up. "Fine. I'm out of it. And the next big-boobed chick that his tongue slips and falls into, I'm gonna let you handle it."

"I made a mistake, Maya," Travis said.

Ugh, my cousin was really working my nerves. Maybe him going back to New York wouldn't be such a bad thing.

"You know what, do whatever. I'm out of it."

"You don't understand," she said.

"You're right. I don't. Because the Sheridan Matthews I know would never let a guy run all over her. But like I said, I'm gonna stay out of it. You do what you have to do."

Travis sat back down on the side of Sheridan and put his arm around her. "That's probably best."

I rolled my eyes at him.

His phone rang. He pulled it and looked at the number, before clicking the button to answer. "Yo, what's up?" he said, like he was thankful for the reprieve. "What?" He lost his smile as he stood and walked away. "Oh, man. Okay, okay, calm down. Chill."

"What?" Sheridan and I asked at the same time.

He turned his back to us. "Are you serious? Oh, no." He paused. "A'ight, a'ight. Chill. Where you at? Which Denny's? Thirty-sixth and what? Nah, I don't know where that is, but

I'll find it. I'm on my way." Travis hung up and ignored our barrage of questions as he raced over to the kitchen counter to get his keys.

"Travis, what's wrong? Where are you going?" I asked.

"Nothing. I'll be back." He headed toward the door.

"Travis," Sheridan said, following him. "You had me come over here and you're just gonna leave?"

"I'm so sorry, Sheridan." He paused. "I wouldn't leave if this wasn't serious."

I had never seen my cousin look so scared. "What do you mean, serious? Where are you going?" His hands were literally shaking. "Travis, tell me what is going on? Is this about drugs?"

"I'll be back" was all he said as he barreled out the door and toward his car.

"Drugs? What are you talking about, drugs?" Sheridan exclaimed.

I ignored her question and simply said, "Let's go."

"Go where? Maya, what is going on?"

"To Denny's on Thirty-sixth. Isn't that where Travis said he was going to meet whoever was on the phone?"

Sheridan looked unsure. "Yeah, but what are we going there for?"

"To find out what is going on and make sure Travis isn't getting caught up in something dangerous."

Sheridan's eyes widened in horror. "Dangerous? What are you talking about?"

I sighed deeply as I snatched open my car door. "Come on. I'll tell you all about it in the car."

Chapter 33

"I cannot believe you have me caught up in some double-oh-seven stuff," Sheridan said as we stayed two cars behind Travis. I had no idea if this really had anything to do with drugs, but the way he had raced out of there, I could tell he was up to something.

We'd followed Travis to the Denny's, where he'd gotten into a black Escalade. He had only been in the truck for about fifteen minutes before he'd gotten out and back into his car. Even though it was getting dark, I could see the terror on his face.

"Just keep up with him," I said. "He's turning!"

Sheridan groaned, but turned as well. "I don't do this kind of stuff." She just kept shaking her head. "I can't believe he's selling drugs. Now you got me in this mess. I don't get down like this," she huffed.

"Yeah, yeah, yeah. In there." I motioned to the upscale apartment building Travis had just turned into.

"Turn the lights off." She rolled her eyes and did as I instructed.

"This doesn't feel right, Maya." I know she was freaking out at everything that I'd just laid on her.

Travis looked frazzled, and the way he darted across the parking lot, I could tell he was up to no good. I almost honked the horn to get him to stop, but I wanted to bust him red-handed so he couldn't lie his way out.

"Come on," I said, opening my car door after we had parked.

"Come on, where?"

"We're going in."

"Unh-unh," she said, locking her door. "You did good getting me this far, but this is where I draw the line. I'm not going in there. It looks like he's involved in something dangerous and I don't do danger."

I blew a deep breath. "Just wait here."

"Maya, don't go in there," she warned. "If Travis really is involved in this K2 ring, you need to let the police handle it."

I turned to her. "Do you want Travis to go to jail?"

"Of course not, but . . ."

"Then I can't go to the cops. Just give me a minute. If I'm not back in thirty minutes, go get some help."

"Go where?" she asked, her eyes wide.

"I don't know, the police, my dad, just whatever." I got out of the car and closed the door on the sound of her voice. Travis had already gone inside. I didn't know how I was going to find him once I got inside the building. But as soon as I looked to the right, I saw his New York Yankees baseball hat bopping down the stairs. I quietly followed, trying to make sure I stayed out of the way. Even though the place was upscale it was dark and eerily quiet. It creeped me out.

Travis went down a long hallway in what looked like a basement area. He stopped outside the door of the last apartment. I went down another hall that thankfully led to the other side so I could peek out and see what was going on.

"Yo, I'm here for Nico," he told the tall, stocky guy standing near the door.

"You got the money?"

"It's on the way. My boy is bringing it."

"Bringing it? Where he at?"

"He's coming. I just—"

He cut Travis off. "Nico said he don't want to see you without your boy."

Now I knew Travis was in trouble. This guy had no-good written all over him. I was just about to come out and let my presence be known when I heard a familiar voice say, "Hold your horses, man. I'm here."

I almost fell over when I noticed Sammy coming down the stairs.

"Man, where you been?" Travis looked so relieved.

"I told you I was on my way. I was trying to take care of that."

"Trying, does that mean you didn't?" Travis was panicked again.

"What did your guy say?" Sammy asked.

Travis just shook his head. Fear covered his face.

"You got the money?" the stocky guy repeated.

Sammy turned to the guy. "Look . . ."

The man started shaking his head. "Naw, naw, wrong answer, bruh. That's a yes-or-no question." He stepped closer. "Do you have the money?"

"Not yet," Sammy said hesitantly.

"That sounds like a no to me. You and your boy here running game on me?"

"Nah, it's not even like that."

I couldn't hold it anymore. I needed to get my cousin—and my man—out of here. "Sammy?" I said, popping up from my hiding spot.

Both Travis and Sammy turned toward me. Travis spoke first. "Maya! What the—"

I cut him off as I stepped in Sammy's face. "I can't believe this!" I told Sammy. I probably should've been afraid but I think I was too mad to even think about it. "So you're a drug dealer, too? Are you the one that got my cousin caught up in this stuff?"

Sammy looked flustered and freaked out. "Maya, it's not even like that. I just didn't want to get you caught up in my business. I'm so sorry I didn't tell you, but I didn't want to involve you."

"Unh-unh, don't be trying to make excuses," I said, waving my finger in his face. I spun on Travis. "And you fixed me up with a freakin' drug dealer? Have you lost your mind?"

"Maya, did you follow me?" Travis asked.

I ignored him and refocused my wrath on Sammy. "You listened to me cry about my cousin and you were the one who got him all involved in this all along."

"Maya, please go. We can talk about this later," Sammy whispered as he tried to push me toward the stairs.

I jerked away from him. "Don't touch me, you liar!"

But before anyone could say another word, the door swung open and a short, thuggish-looking man in a linen button-down shirt and matching pants stood there. He had tiny dreads and a gold tooth.

"See, this is that mess I'm talking about. Y'all bring this to my doorstep?" he said, angrily.

It was then that I noticed the small chrome pistol that the bodyguard near the door was pointing at us.

"Tell you what. Why don't you all bring this little family reunion inside and tell Papa Nico what's really going on?"

Chapter 34

"This has nothing to do with her. Let her go," Travis said as the three of us sat side by side on the plush leather sofa inside the luxurious apartment. You'd never know from outside the building that something like this was inside. This apartment was fiyah!

"Yes, she didn't have anything to do with this," Sammy added.

Nico shook his head. "Sorry, pretty lady. When you stick your nose in other people's business, then you have something to do with this."

"Look, Nino," I began.

He shot me a crazy look. "Nino?"

"Like Nino, from that drug movie, *New Jack City.*"

"Nico, the name is *Nico.*"

"Okay, Mr. Nico. I was just here to grab my cousin. If I could just get him and my boyfriend"—I glared at Sammy—"I mean, my ex-boyfriend, we'll be out. I don't want any trouble."

Nico burst out laughing, then turned to the guy who had been by the door. "You hear that, Lex? She wants to just get her cousin and her man and they gon' be out. That's all she wants."

Sammy stood up. "Come on, Nico. This is just between us."

Nico lost his smile and held up his hand. "You would *not* want to talk to me, son. Unless you're sayin' to me, 'I got your money,' there's nothin' you need to be saying to me." Sammy slid back into his seat as Nico took a deep breath to calm himself before turning back to me. "What's your name, doll baby?"

I frowned at him. "It sure isn't doll baby."

"Maya, chill," Travis hissed in my direction.

I mean, don't get me wrong, I was scared, but he still needed to get my name right.

"Do you know who I am?" I said, thinking maybe if Nico knew whom he was dealing with, he'd let us go.

"No, enlighten me."

Travis grabbed my arm as if he was trying to shut me up. I ignored him and continued. "I'm Maya Morgan."

"Oooooh, snap," Nico said. "That makes all the difference in the world. Why didn't you tell me that's who you were?" He stopped and stared at me. "Who in world is Maya Morgan?"

"She does a gossip show on TV." We all turned toward the feminine voice coming from the doorway I looked up to see a leggy woman in a super tight miniskirt, her blond hair hanging down her back. She was smacking on a piece of gum like she had been a cow in a former life.

I nodded. "That's me."

"How old are you?" Nico asked.

"Eighteen."

"She's seventeen," Travis said. "And she isn't in this."

"You told me you weren't in it either," I snapped.

"Maya . . . ," Sammy said.

I gave him the hand. "I'm with Nico. You don't need to be talking to me. You were just playing me when all along—

you're the one got him selling these drugs. Are you even a record producer?"

The way he lowered his eyes answered my question.

"What? You took me to your studio."

Nico laughed. "Jax told me you brought some chick over there to impress her, acting like you was running stuff. Boy, you got game."

I was horrified. "That was lie? You were just pretending? Oh my God. I can't believe you." I actually hit him on the shoulder as I jumped up from my seat.

Nico turned and looked at Lex. "Is this really going on? I run a multimillion-dollar business and I got a crazy cousin, a lying boyfriend, and a baby mama going at it in my living room. Like for real?"

"Oh, hold on," I screamed. "I am not anyone's baby mama!"

"This not your baby's mama?" he asked Sammy.

I spun on to Sammy. "You got a baby mama?"

He let out a long sigh. "Maya, I wanted to tell you, but . . ."

"Oh, my, God, I can't believe this!" I shouted. "Is your name even Sammy?" I punched him again. "You are such a freaking liar!" Then, I turned and punched Travis. "And how are you gonna have me hooking up with someone like this!"

Travis grabbed his arm. "I told you not to get serious. He was just somebody to kick it with."

I hit Travis again. "You are out of order for fixing me up with him in the first place! I can't believe this!"

"I can't believe none of this," Nico said, shaking his head.

I snapped my head in Nico's direction and gave him the hand. "Shhh. I will get with you in a minute." I turned back to Sammy. I knew I wasn't thinking straight to be talking to a drug kingpin like that, but I couldn't believe all of Sammy's lies. "Do you or do you not have a baby mama?" I asked him.

"Did she just shush me?" Nico asked in disbelief.

Lex laughed. "Yeah, boss. I think she did."

"You know, all of this *Young and the Restless* stuff, yeah, not feeling it." Nico stepped toward me and I stopped going off. For now. But I glared at him. We stood eye to eye until he finally said, "I like you." He leaned in to my ear. "That feistiness turns me on." His breath smelled like old cigars. "You need to leave these boys alone and come play with the big dogs. I can buy you whatever you want." He motioned to the ghetto girl in the corner. "Ask her."

My hands went to my hips. "*I* can buy me whatever I want."

Nico started laughing. It was at that point when I noticed the hoochie standing off in the corner was getting mad. She stood with her arms folded across her chest. "Really, Nico?"

"Come on, Margarita. Don't start trippin'. Go on upstairs and wait on me."

She glared at him, shot me an ugly look, then turned and bounced back up the stairs.

Nico didn't pay her any more attention as he turned back to us. "Look, I'm about tired of all of this," he said.

"Cool. We'll just get out of here then," Sammy said, standing up and trying to take my hand. Of course, I snatched it away. "I'll get your money by tomorrow," Sammy said.

"I know you gon' get my money," Nico said, grabbing my arm and jerking me toward him. "And I'm gonna hold on to your little girlfriend until you do."

"What?" I said, trying to snatch my arm away from him, too. But his grip was tight and I couldn't get my arm back. "Are you crazy? I'm not staying here. Let go of me."

He shook me. "Look, little girl, I'm tired of playing with you. It was cute at first, but now you're just working my nerves. And since you want to stick your nose all up in my business, I'm gonna keep you around for collateral."

The look in his eyes told me he was serious and it was time out for joking.

Travis actually charged in his direction, but Lex immediately stepped up and pointed a pistol at his head, stopping him in his tracks.

The other bodyguard, who had come to the door with Nico, and who'd been standing quietly in the back this whole time, pulled out his gun as well. Travis quickly retreated.

Nico's grip on me tightened as he laughed. "Ah, ah, ah. I wouldn't do that if I were you. My man gets trigger-happy when someone gets too close to me." He pulled me in front of him in a bear hug. "And I'd hate to have him splatter your blood all over this pretty lady's outfit."

Now, I was for-real shaking.

"Sammy, you'd better tell your boy here what happened to the last little dude that tried to run up on me," Nico said.

Sammy didn't say a word, but grabbed Travis's arm and pulled him back.

"Please, Mr. Nico. Let me go," I cried.

He put his hand over my mouth to shut me up, which scared me even more.

"Come on, man, please?" I could see the fear in Travis's eyes. "I told you she has nothing to do with this!"

"Give me my money and this is all over," Nico calmly said as he removed his hand from my mouth.

"Just give him the money back," I told Sammy when neither of them moved. He and Travis exchanged looks.

"We don't have it," Sammy finally said.

"What do you mean you don't have it?"

"We got robbed," Sammy said.

"Now that sounds like a personal problem," Nico replied.

"Look, Mr. Nico. I got plenty of money. How much do they owe you?" I reached in my bag that was strapped around my body. "I have an American Express black card and you can just charge whatever they owe."

Nico looked at Lex and they both just burst out laughing. "I'm sorry, our credit card machine is down today," Nico said.

"Yeah," Lex added. "We need our two hundred and fifty in cash?"

"Two hundred and fifty?" Sammy exclaimed.

"Yeah," Lex replied, "that includes interest."

"Why didn't you just say that?" I said, reaching in my purse again. "Here, do you have change?" I said, handing him three one-hundred-dollar bills.

They busted out laughing again. "Girl, you funny." Nico laughed, then lost his smile. "Two hundred and fifty G's."

"What?" I screamed. "Travis, what were you doing messing around with that kind of money?"

"It wasn't but a hundred and fifty worth of drugs," Sammy protested.

"Hey, compounded interest," Nico said. "You were supposed to have my money yesterday. You didn't, so now you gotta pay the interest." He shrugged.

"Come on, man," Sammy pleaded. "You said we were partners."

Nico laughed. "And you believed me?" He smiled like he was really proud of himself. "You young bucks really are stupid. But look here, I'm tired of talking. Get my money."

"I told you, we were robbed," Sammy said.

"And I told you, not my problem. I ain't playing around. You want me to believe somebody robbed you? Please. So, here's how it's going to work." He grabbed my arm and pulled me toward him. "I'm gonna hold on to shorty here while the two of you go get my money."

"No, I'm leaving!" I squirmed, trying to get away.

"Nah, I don't think so," Nico said. He kissed my neck. I wanted to throw up. "Now, I'm not gonna hurt you, yet," he said. "But I'm gonna keep you here until these fellas come back with my money." He narrowed his eyes in their direction. "And if you go to the cops, I'm gonna make sure she dies," he said, squeezing me tighter. "Then I'm gonna make sure your real baby mama and your baby die," he said, looking at Sammy. "And you," he added, turning to Travis, "I'm gonna get someone up in Brooklyn to take care of that fine mama of yours."

How does he know about Aunt Bev? It was at that moment when I realized Travis really was in this thing deep. And now, it looked like I was, too.

"My . . . my friend is outside," I stammered, suddenly remembering Sheridan. "She's probably calling the cops right now."

Nico studied me like he was trying to see if I was telling the truth.

"Joe, go handle that," he finally said to the bodyguard in the corner.

I grimaced, hoping he didn't hurt her.

"Okay, but let Travis and Maya go. I'm the one that was robbed. I'll handle it," Sammy said.

"Lil dude, I'm done talking," Nico replied.

"But . . ."

"But nothing. Be gone," he said, waving them off.

"No!" I screamed. I actually was able to squirm out of his grip, but he grabbed me by my hair and tossed me down in a chair.

"Chill out, little girl. Make yourself comfortable. You gon' be here a minute."

"And lil G," he said, pointing at Travis, "don't be stupid. You get five-o involved, I'm just gonna have to put a bullet in her pretty little head." He stroked my hair.

I swallowed hard and fought to keep the tears back. I don't think I'd ever been as scared as I was at that very moment.

"It's okay, cuz," Travis said, his voice shaking. "I'll get the money."

"Babe, we're coming back. I promise," Sammy said.

I didn't want to talk to either one of them, but I was so scared, all I could do was say, "Just hurry." I looked at Travis. "And please, check on Sheridan. Make sure that guy didn't do anything to her."

"Let's go," Lex said, pushing them out the door. I just prayed that wasn't my last time seeing them.

Chapter 35

This was a bad dream. A really, really bad dream. That was the only thing I could think as I sat trying to figure out how I had ended up here. All I'd wanted to do was keep my cousin out of danger. I never imagined I'd end up in the middle of danger right there with him.

But my mind couldn't even process all of that because I was absolutely floored about Sammy. Now that I thought about it, I should've known. He was too well-connected. Him and his private singers who didn't want people around. My never being able to go to his house. The crackhead uncle who blamed him. The ex-girlfriend who asked if I knew what he did. He probably lived with his baby mama.

I just couldn't believe this. *Maya Morgan dating a drug dealer?* Ugh. It made my skin crawl. And so did the drug dealer of all drug dealers sitting in front of me.

"Why you staring at me like that, baby girl?" Nico asked.

"Maya. The name is Maya."

"You sure got a lot of balls, little girl." He looked at Lex. "Okay, I get she didn't know who I was in the beginning, but even when I told her, it was like she wasn't backing down."

Lex chuckled, as did the quiet bodyguard. I was starting to wonder why he was even here. He'd barely uttered two words and it was like he stayed in the background.

"So, I guess you're not scared of me?" Nico asked.

"Oh no, trust, you terrify me," I said calmly. "But that still doesn't mean I'm going to let you disrespect me."

Nico smiled, like he was proud of me or something. "I like a woman that's feisty."

Margarita, who was sitting in the corner flipping through a magazine, looked up and scowled. I was beginning to wonder why she was with this guy. He treated her like crap and completely disrespected her in front of everybody. She was decent-looking, so it couldn't have been a self-esteem issue. It had to be the money. She dressed like new money. Real new, like "I won the lotto yesterday."

"Margarita, you can take some lessons from her," Nico said.

She clicked her teeth and wiggled her head. "I don't need to take no lessons from nobody. And I tell you about yourself all the time."

"Yeah, you do." Nico laughed as he turned to Lex. "But all I gotta do is toss a hundred at her, and she'll be like a dang lapdog."

Margarita continued glaring at Nico as he and Lex continued laughing.

"Well, you can throw all the money at me you want, but you will still respect me." I folded my arms. I was done talking to him.

"What you do again?" he asked me.

I just glared at him. I wanted to tell him it was none of his business, but I decided to just stay quiet.

"Oh, so now you not talking to me?" he said. When I didn't answer, he picked his gun up. "I'm gonna repeat, what do you do?"

I may have been feisty, but I wasn't stupid. "I'm in school."

"Oooh, a smart girl, too. Beauty and brains. Where you go to college?"

"Not college. High school."

He looked shocked. "Dang. You still in high school?" His eyes ran up and down my body. "Man, you some serious jail bait. You gonna get some dudes locked up."

I rolled my eyes. "How long do you plan on keeping me here?"

He leaned back, turning serious. "You heard. Til your boys get back here with my money."

"I didn't have anything to do with your money."

"Yeah, but you ever heard of collateral damage?"

I sighed heavily. "I work in television. I'm supposed to go to work tomorrow. My boss will be looking for me. And if I don't come home, my mom will have the SWAT team out looking for me."

Nico leaned in. "Little girl, don't try to run game on me."

I paused. My mom had actually left yesterday for a shopping trip to Argentina, but I needed him to think someone would be looking for me. "My parents check in with me every night."

Nico was thinking. I was hoping that would help him come to his senses.

"Plus, my friend Sheridan knows where I was," I added.

"Oh, was that the chick outside?" he asked Joe, who nodded. Nico turned back to me. "Oh, we got Sheridan taken care of."

My eyes widened. What did that mean? Oh my God, if something had happened to Sheridan . . .

Joe must've read the look on my face because he said, "Chill, she a'ight. She's gonna keep her mouth closed."

Nico shot him a look, and he stepped back like he shouldn't have said anything.

I could only imagine the terror Sheridan was going through right now.

"But you know, you got a point, baby girl." He handed me his cell phone. "Call your mama and tell her you won't be home tonight."

"You definitely don't know my mom. That's not gonna fly."

"Just do it," Nico hissed. I could tell he was no longer playing around so I slowly took the phone. "Tell her you're about to turn in for the night. Hopefully, you'll be home safe and sound before she gets back in town. Then, you call your job and tell them you're sick and won't be in or some other lie. You lie for a living."

"I don't lie!"

"Rumors, lies, it's all the same. Make the call."

"Really, Nico? The number will show up if she uses your phone," Margarita huffed like he hadn't thought this through.

Nico looked over at her, then at Lex. "See, this is why I keep her around, because she thinks of things I'm obviously too dumb to think about." He spun back to Margarita. "Keep your nose out of my business. Like I'm gonna let someone use my phone if my number would show up. You dumb broad, I don't need your input. Just sit over there and shut up and try to look cute." He looked at her in disgust. "You don't even do that anymore."

Margarita glared at him as her eyes filled with tears.

I took the phone and slowly dialed my mom's number.

"Put it on speakerphone," Nico said.

I did as he said, and waited while it rang. "Hey, Mom?" I said when she answered.

"How are you, sweetie? Argentina is beautiful. I should've brought you so we could go shopping together. Your dad gave me the black card." She giggled.

I wanted to scream. *I'm being kidnapped and you're talking about shopping in Argentina!*

I sighed as Nico gave me the sign to wrap up. "Well, I was just checking in. I'm going to bed. You know, in case you decided to call."

"Okay, honey."

"I mean, I just wanted to tell you if you call, you won't be able to get me," I continued. I couldn't believe this. Wasn't there supposed to be some kind of mental mother-daughter bond that could tell her when I was in trouble?

"Okay, sweet dreams. Gotta go," my mom said. "My tour guide is here. Don't tell your father, but he is so fabulous. Love you." She hung the phone up and I swear, I wanted to cry.

"Dang, sounds like moms is a piece of work," Nico said. "Now, call your job."

I dialed Tamara's personal cell phone. I was sick when it went to her voice mail.

"Leave a message," Nico mouthed.

"Hey Tamara, it's Maya," I slowly began. "I'm not feeling well. I won't be in today. . . ."

"Or tomorrow," he whispered.

"Or tomorrow," I repeated. "Okay. Bye."

I hoped that she recognized how strange this message was. At this point, I just didn't know. At this point, I didn't know anything, including whether I'd even make it out alive.

Chapter 36

I couldn't make out the look on Travis's face. All I knew was this wasn't looking good. And I couldn't figure out why my cousin was here by himself. If Sammy had gotten him into this mess, Sammy needed to be here with him.

"You got my money?"

"Look, Nico." Travis nervously sighed. "We didn't get it all."

"Then why are you here?" He slowly lit his cigar.

Travis tossed a small duffel bag at Nico's feet. "Here's ten grand. I just need one more day."

Nico snatched the bag up and pulled out a stack of bills. "Ten thousand dollars? I blow my nose with this."

"Come on, Nico, man," Travis pleaded.

Nico slowly inhaled, then blew a ring of smoke. "Where's your partner at?"

"He's working to get the rest of the money. We just wanted to show you that we are serious. Can you please let my cousin go?"

"Now, you know that's not gonna happen, young bruh." Nico glanced down at the money, over at me, then back at Travis. "But since I am in a giving mood"—he stuffed some of the money in his pocket—"I'm going to go ahead and give you another twenty-four hours. But after that, it's bye-bye, Betty." He motioned in my direction.

"My name is Maya," I snapped.

"Can somebody get a muzzle for this chick?" he said like he was irritated with me.

"If I'm getting on your nerves, I'd be happy to leave," I couldn't help but say.

That made him laugh as he walked over and squeezed my chin so tight it hurt. "Your feistiness ain't cute no more. And right now, you easing onto my bad side." He pushed me down on the sofa by my chin. "So sit down and shut up! You ain't goin' nowhere 'til I get my money." He turned back to Travis. "All of it."

I tried to get up, but Travis gave me a "please chill" look.

"Yo, Nico. Can I talk to my cousin just for a minute? She's really scared. I'll calm her down."

Nico glared at me but didn't respond.

"Come on, Nico," Margarita said, stepping up. I didn't even know that she'd come into the room. "You can let them talk. It's not like either of them is dumb enough to try anything with all these bodyguards around. She's just a kid."

I wanted to ask Margarita who she was calling a kid, but I figured now wasn't the time.

"Fine. All this mushy crap getting on my nerves."

He went and sat in the big recliner in the corner and continued smoking his cigar.

Travis helped me up off the sofa and pulled me to the side. "How you doin', Maya?" he gently asked.

"I'm having a great day, Travis. How do you think I'm doin'?" I snapped. Tears actually started forming in my eyes.

"Did you find Sheridan?"

Travis nodded. "Joe, Nico's bodyguard, made her leave. He told her to wait to hear from me but not to call the police. She was scared to death, but she did as he said. Now, she's freaking out with worry."

"Yeah, me too."

"This will be over soon." He hugged me.

I wish I could say that I felt safe in his arms, but I wouldn't feel safe until I was out of this place. "Where did you get the money from?" I asked.

"I sold my father's watch."

My heart dropped. "What? But that meant the world to you."

"You mean more to me, Maya. I'm so, so sorry I got you caught up in this."

I no longer felt like beating him up. I just wanted to get out of there. "Travis, look. Just go ask my dad for the money."

He shook his head like that wasn't an option. "What do you think Uncle Myles is gonna do? Do you think he's going to pay up?"

"You know he will give it to you."

"No, he won't. He's gonna go straight to the cops. And for real, Nico doesn't play. If he even thinks some cops are involved, he's killin' everybody. I can't take that chance."

I couldn't help but wonder if this was more about him than me. Travis wouldn't want to tell my dad because my dad would kill him first, then go to the cops. "Well, I have some money in my savings. It's not two hundred and fifty thousand, but it'll help."

"And how am I supposed to get that?"

"Maybe he'll let me go get the money and come back." Even as I said it, I knew Nico wasn't going to go for that.

"Just hang tight, okay? Sammy had some money stashed and he's using that and he has a lead on the guys who robbed him."

We stopped talking as Nico headed our way. "A'ight, enough." He pulled me back toward him again. "Go get the rest of my money, and this time, don't come back here without it."

Chapter 37

My mind was wandering. I wondered if Tamara was looking for me. I knew she'd been calling me, even though Nico had my phone. Tamara wasn't the type to buy that "I'm sick" story without suspecting something. I wondered if she would try to call my parents. I wondered what Travis was doing. How he was going to get the money. I hoped he didn't steal anything from my dad, but if he did, I wouldn't blame him. At this point he needed to do whatever he needed to do to get me out of this situation.

"Margarita, keep her entertained," Nico said, sliding a gun across the table to her.

I looked at the hoochie sitting across the room and glaring at me like I wanted to be here or something.

"What you looking at?" she said, wiggling her neck.

"Is your name really Margarita?" I asked.

"Yeah, and?"

"And, no reason really." I paused. "I mean, that's like the name you born with? Like your mom took one look at you and said, 'Oooh, she look like a Margarita.'"

Nico burst out laughing again. "I love this chick. I need

someone like her in my life," he added before disappearing up the stairs.

Margarita, meanwhile, didn't see anything funny.

I watched the TV for a few minutes. *Maury* was on. Even though the volume was muted, I could tell by the way some woman was sobbing as she ran off the stage that the man next to her was not the father.

I couldn't believe Margarita was really into this mess.

Finally, I couldn't take the silence anymore. "So are you Nico's girlfriend?"

"I sure am," she answered with an attitude. "And don't come up in here trying to get with my man."

Is she for real? I couldn't help but look at her like she was crazy. "Yeah, you don't have to worry about me. I just want to get out of here." I glanced around the room. "Look, if you let me go, I promise I won't say anything."

"Girl, you got me messed up," she said. "Do you see this fly outfit I got on?" I swear, although she was pretty, she sounded just like Sheneneh from the show *Martin*. "This is Chanel, baby," she added as she ran her hands up and down her too-tight outfit.

I didn't know Chanel made hoochie.

"And do you see these earrings?" She pointed to her ears. "Diamonds, boo boo. So if Nico say you gon' sit here, you gon' sit here."

I considered charging her, but since she was sitting there with her hand on the pistol—not to mention she looked like she was straight out of the hood—I didn't even want to chance it.

"What you doing around here anyway?" she asked.

"I was just following my cousin," I said. "I knew he was up to something and I was trying to find out what was going on."

"Ummm-hmmm," Margarita said. "That's why you need

to be minding your own business. That's what my mama always said, at least before she got locked up."

"Is that what you do with Nico, mind your own business?" I asked.

"I sure do," she replied. "Ain't no shame in my game. As long as he takes care of me, he can handle his business."

"Wow. Do you mind if ask how old you are?"

"You so nosey," she said.

I shrugged and gave her a "what can I say?" look.

"I'm twenty-two," she replied.

"And you don't want more in life?"

"What more is there to want?" She waved around the apartment. "I got it all."

"Okay, if you say so."

"Why you ask so many questions?"

"I just do. Seriously, you like the way he treats you?"

I don't know why I was getting all up in her business, but I needed something to pass the time. If I sat here just thinking, I'd start planning my demise, and I didn't need to be thinking about that.

"Nico buys me nice stuff."

"I didn't ask you what he buys you."

"Don't worry about the way Nico treats me."

"Cool." I swallowed hard as I struggled to say what I wanted to say next. "It's just, if I was as pretty as you, I'd be having dudes crawling at my feet, not the other way around."

She stopped and looked at me. "You think I'm pretty?"

"Yeah, you're gorgeous. And I don't mean that in a freaky sort of way," I felt the need to add.

She sat like she was thinking. "I told Nico if he didn't start treating me better, I was going to find someone who would."

"You should," I said, trying to egg her on. "You remind me of those trophy chicks professional athletes have on their arms. They treat them well and shower them with gifts because they know if they don't, another dude will." I wanted to gas her up in hopes that I could get her to help me escape. "That's the life you should have."

She nodded like she couldn't agree more. "That's what I'm talking about." She paused like she was thinking. "Nico used to be nice, back when he was trying to get with me."

"What happened?"

She shrugged. "He started working for this big-time dude, who pumped even more money in his pocket and he got the big head."

That made me sit up and take notice as I suddenly remembered that phone call I'd gotten at the station.

"Oh, yeah, I heard about that guy."

Her eyes widened. "You have?"

"Yeah, I know he's the one behind the whole operation."

Margarita looked over her shoulder, toward the door, then back at me. "Shhh, girl. You betta not let Nico hear you say that. He guards Donovan like he's Jesus or something."

Donovan? Donovan? OMG, no way was she talking about Donovan Davis. He was one of Hollywood's hottest stars back in the nineties, but he'd fallen off and hadn't been doing much lately—just like the caller had said. That had to be who she was talking about because Donovan lived in Miami. I'd heard rumors he was involved with drugs, but I would've never taken him for the kingpin of it all.

I lowered my voice. "Good looking out. I just was trippin' over why Donovan would be dealing. I mean, he's loaded from all those movies he made."

"He also lost a lot of money from gambling. Then, apparently, he hooked up with someone in South America that set him up with some drugs and he got caught up in the money." She looked sad for a minute. "We all did, I guess."

"Yeah, but it's not right that he's sitting back and playing his Hollywood role and he got Nico doing all the dirty work."

Margarita slapped the table. "That's what I've been telling Nico."

"Maybe you can get through to him," I said.

"Please, Nico don't listen to nobody."

Just then, her phone chirped. She picked it up, read the text message, and frowned. "This trick right here . . . ," she mumbled, tossing the phone back on the table.

"What's wrong?"

She hesitated, like she wasn't sure if she should be telling me. "That's Nico's baby mama. I can't stand that tramp. She just sent me a text, talking about Nico on his way to see her."

I reached across the table and touched Margarita's hand. "Girl, you deserve better." I no longer was gassing her up. I didn't know Margarita, but she definitely deserved better.

Margarita looked like she was thinking, but then quickly snatched her hand away when Nico walked back in the room.

Nico eyed me suspiciously. "What y'all doing?"

"Nothing," she said, nervously. "I'm just watching her like you told me to."

"Well, watch her for a little while longer. Bull is upstairs, so if you need anything just holler. Joe and Lex are going with me."

"Where you goin'?" Margarita asked.

He looked irritated, like he didn't like being questioned. "Out."

"Out where?"

He blew a frustrated breath. "Dang, girl, who you think you are questioning me?"

Margarita stood up, and I could see her eyes watering up. "You're going over Shebrina's house, aren't you?"

Nico glared at her for a minute. I just knew he was going to keep denying it, but he said. "Okay, and so what? I want to see my son."

"Did you forget? Your son ain't even there. He's with She-brina's father." She poked her lips out like she was really mad.

"What, you keeping tabs on my kids now?"

I couldn't believe I was sitting here watching this mess like it was some kind of ghetto reality show.

"Nico, the last time you went over there, you spent the night."

He waved her off and headed toward the door. She followed him and grabbed his arm. "Please don't go." I wanted to grab Margarita and shake some sense into her. I couldn't believe she was begging a guy.

Nico pushed her so hard she fell to the ground. "I told you about putting your hands on me!" Then, while Margarita lay on the ground, he took his right foot and kicked her in the side. "I told your behind to stop being such a nag!"

Margarita screamed as he kicked her again. I grimaced in horror. Joe stepped up. "Yo, boss, let's roll."

Nico looked down at Margarita and shook his head. "Shoot, on the real, you might need to be taking some lessons from Shebrina on how to be a real woman."

With that, he turned and stomped out of the apartment.

Chapter 38

I just didn't get girls who cried their eyes out behind some guy. Bryce had done me dirty, and I really had loved him. But at the end of the day, it was his loss that he had messed things up with me. So the last thing I'd ever do was sit up and bawl like a baby behind him. Yes, I'd shed a tear or two, but I definitely wouldn't do it in front of somebody like Margarita was sitting up here doing now.

"Why don't you just leave him?" I asked.

"Why don't you just mind your business?" she snapped, dabbing her eyes.

I put my hands up in defense. "My bad. I'm just trying to look out for you."

We sat in silence for a few minutes. Then I said, "So, you're willing to go to jail for him?"

She frowned at me. "What is that supposed to mean?"

"Just what I said. You a ride-or-die chick and don't mind if that ride takes you to prison?"

"What are you talking about? I don't sell drugs."

"Yeah, but you're a kidnapper."

She looked at me confused. "I'm not a kidnapper."

I looked at her, looked at the gun. "So that means I'm free to leave?"

That made her nervous. She squeezed the gun. "Look, just sit there till Nico gets back. You can't go nowhere."

"Yeah, that sounds like I'm being held against my will and the last time I checked, that's the definition of kidnapping."

"You ain't no kid!"

"Technically, I am. I'm only seventeen." I didn't think I'd ever have admitted anything like that, but I was at the point where I wanted to try whatever worked.

I shook my head at her logic, but I could tell from the way she was getting all worked up that her mind wasn't focused on me anyway, so I just left it alone. We sat again in silence until I could no longer help myself.

"So, what do you think Nico is doing with his baby's mama right now?" I asked.

She slammed her hand on the table again. Luckily, it wasn't the hand gripping the gun. "Shut up!"

I knew I was pushing my luck, but this was my only chance. "I'm just saying, you said his son was out of town. You think Shebrina is gonna let him drop off some money without properly thanking him?"

"Shut up," she repeated. This time she pointed the gun at me. Her hand was shaking so I just said, "Okay, fine."

She finally lowered the gun and just cried and cried and cried. Then, she got up grabbed her cell phone and walked over to the corner. She made a phone call, crying the whole time. I guess she was crying on one of her friends' shoulders. After about ten minutes, she came back to the table and cried some more. It was really exhausting.

Meanwhile, I sat there trying to figure out how the heck I was going to get out of here. I couldn't sit around and wait on Travis and Sammy because I wasn't convinced they would come up with the money. My mom and dad would kill Travis if he went to them, and they were out of town, anyway.

Margarita continued sniffling, gun in one hand, tissues in the other. I was surprised, though, when after about twenty minutes, I heard a light snoring. Had she seriously fallen asleep? What kind of criminals were these?

I eased out of my seat, remembering that Bull was still upstairs. I made my way over to the door, then silently cursed when I noticed the burglar bars. There was no way I'd be able to get out of there. I glanced around. There were burglar bars on the windows as well. The only thing I could do was try to find the key.

I knew I had to act fast because it was only a matter of time before Bull came downstairs, or Margarita woke up, or worse, Nico returned.

I tiptoed around, looking for the key. I spotted a window where there were no burglar bars. It was like one of those skylights up near the ceiling. I quietly moved the chair over and climbed on top. I had just eased the window open, when my other foot caused the chair to topple over.

The noise instantly woke up Margarita. "Hey, what are you doing?" she yelled, racing over to the window.

I panicked and kicked the screen with all my might. It fell off and I had just gotten one foot out the window right when Margarita got to me. I didn't know if she would actually shoot me or what. So when I felt her grab my leg as she shouted, "Get back in here," I kicked her as hard as I could. She yelped and fell down, and I scrambled out the window. It was at that point that I noticed the window was several floors up and I'd have to jump if I wanted to get out.

"Bull! Help!" Margarita screamed. I knew that meant it was now or never, so I took a deep breath and jumped. I hit the ground with a thud and grimaced in pain as my leg twisted underneath me. Still, I managed to pull myself up. I had just gotten up when a silver Bentley pulled up and Nico jumped out.

I tried to take off running, but Lex jumped out as well and caught me before I made it to the sidewalk. He had me up like I was a rag doll.

"Let me go! Let me go!" I screamed, flailing my arms as I tried to hit and kick him. It didn't do any good, though. The guy was three times my size and I couldn't break free. He picked me up under one arm and carried me back inside.

By now, I was in tears. Just as he reached the front door, Margarita swung the door open and unlocked the burglar bars. Bull was right behind her. Her eyes widened in horror as she stood face-to-face with Nico.

"Baby, I am so sorry," she immediately began crying. "She just—"

But before she could finish her sentence, Nico reached back and slapped her as hard as he could. "I can't trust you to do nothing!" he spat. "And Bull, what you doing?"

"Boss, I was upstairs. You told me to stay up there unless something was wrong."

"Obviously something was wrong!"

Bull was speechless. Nico pushed him aside and stomped in. Lex followed, then threw me down onto the sofa.

Margarita actually struggled to get up off the ground. "I told you, don't put your hands on me again," she cried, charging at him like a raging bull. I guess she was fed up with him.

Nico punched her before she made contact, making her fall back down. "Do you think I care what you told me!" he yelled.

I actually felt bad for her. She was sobbing uncontrollably as blood seeped from her nose.

He spun back toward me. "Now you, little girl, you got one more time to try me. I have no problem bustin' a cap in that pretty little head of yours, then waiting until your cousin and boyfriend get here, then busting a cap in them as well. Ya feel me?"

I nodded as I sniffed. After the beat down he'd just put on Margarita, I knew what he was capable of.

Nico looked down at Margarita, who was still bleeding from the nose. Mascara was running down her face. There was a big shoe print on her beige dress from where he'd stomped her.

"Go get yourself cleaned up," he told her. "You look a hot mess." He shook his head. "Man, I need a drink. I should've stayed over Shebrina's house for all of this."

"Keep this girl under control," he told Joe as he stormed out of the room.

Joe came over to me and tried to gently pat my hand. "Just be cool. It's going to be okay, okay?" he said softly.

I snatched my hand away. I wanted to know how he'd feel about being held against his will. But I didn't say a word, I just sat there praying that Travis, Sammy, my dad, or even the police, *somebody*, would show up soon and put an end to this nightmare.

Chapter 39

They'd done it. They'd really done it. Travis and Sammy were standing in Nico's living room with what I assumed was a duffel bag full of money. Of course, I'd hoped that they'd be able to get the money, but honestly I just hadn't thought it was going to be possible.

"Frisk them," Nico said, motioning in their direction. "I need to make sure they aren't trying any funny stuff like setting me up or something."

"Come on, Nico, we wouldn't do that," Sammy said as Lex started patting him down.

"Not if you have any sense you won't," Nico replied.

Travis was literally shivering as Joe patted him up and down. I glanced over just as Margarita eased into the room.

"He's clean," Lex said.

"Him, too," Joe added.

Sammy and Travis stood there as he moved out of the way and Nico stepped forward. Travis looked unusually nervous, and it had me scared. I couldn't believe that he'd managed to get the rest of the money. At first, I'd thought he would go ahead and get it from my dad, but my dad would be here with the police if he had.

Lex handed Nico the duffel bag. "It's all there, boss."

I tried to gauge why Travis was so nervous. Finally, I chalked it up to this whole situation. Nico was enough to scare the crap out of anyone.

Nico opened the bag and peered in. "I knew there was a reason I liked you, young bucks."

Nico took a stack of money and flipped through the bills. He leaned in and sniffed the snack. "Umph, my favorite smell. Y'all sure you don't want to keep working for me?"

"We told you we want out of the game," Sammy said.

"But, Sammy," Nico said, taking a step toward him, "you've blown up so. All the stars know your name. You run in top-notch circles." He glanced over at me. "You hook up with hot chicks." He patted Sammy's cheek. "How you think you did all that? Me, that's how."

"Yeah, but I was just a front." Sammy had the nerve to sound mad about it.

"Hey, that's how you play the game, young buck. Don't you know rule number one of the ol' G handbook? You get you a wet-behind-the-ears kid who craves the whole money, power, respect thing—even though he hasn't yet earned it. Let him be the face of the business, so when he goes down, your hands are clean."

Sammy looked like he wanted to clock Nico in the eye. "Whatever, Nico. Can we just get Maya and go?"

"I don't know. I like having her around. I might need to make her one of my girls." He looked at Margarita, who was standing off to the side, glaring at him. "It might be time for me to upgrade. Take the old garbage out and get me a new and improved model."

Margarita took a step to him. "I got your old garbage," she said.

"Trick, be gone," he said, pushing her so hard she fell to the floor. I immediately raced to her side.

"Margarita, it's gonna be okay," I said.

Tears filled her eyes, but she refused to let them fall. "Don't worry about me. He's gon' get his."

"Who gon' give it to me?" He motioned to Lex. "Get this trick out my house."

Margarita was screaming and cussing as Lex picked her up and carried her to the door. He opened the door and tossed her out. I felt so bad for her. But just as Lex was about to close the door behind her, it suddenly swung open, startling everyone.

"Police, freeze!"

"What the—!" Nico immediately dove behind the sofa. "Y'all set me up?" he screamed.

"No!" Travis yelled, his hands going up in the air.

But Nico wasn't hearing anything. He opened fire as I scrambled behind the sofa. If I had been thinking clearly, I would've run toward the door. But when bullets are whizzing by, you run for the first cover you can get. It was a bad move because just as I got behind the sofa, my eyes met Nico's, and before I could run, he grabbed me. "You gon' be my insurance that I get out here."

I screamed as he put his arm around my neck and the gun to my head, and pulled me up.

"Back off!" he yelled.

Sammy saw me and charged toward Nico. "Let her go!"

Nico pulled the trigger. I swear, everything seemed to go in slow motion as the bullet tore into Sammy, knocking him back against the living room wall.

Tears were streaming down my face as I tried to squirm free. I just knew this was about to be the end. Nico was panicking. Cops were yelling, and he had the cold steel pointed at my head.

But just then, I heard, "Drop your gun, Nico. It's over."

Both Nico and I turned to see Joe standing there with a gun pointed right at Nico's head.

"Joe?" Nico said. It was enough of a distraction for Joe to

disarm Nico and push him to the floor. I took my chance and ran across the room to the nearest policeman.

"Man, what you doing?" Nico asked, shocked.

"What I been waiting to do a long time." Joe pulled out a badge and flashed it at Nico. "Nico Caruthers, you have the right to remain silent. Anything you say can and will be used against you . . ."

"You're a cop?" Nico yelled.

"You have the right to an attorney . . ."

"Don't you know who I am?"

"Yeah, you're under arrest!" Joe said as he finished reading Nico his rights.

"I told y'all no cops," Nico spat in Sammy and Travis's direction. "You're gonna regret it."

"We didn't do it," Travis protested.

"They didn't," Margarita said, reappearing in the doorway. "I did."

Nico looked confused.

"Thanks for all your help, Margarita," Joe said as he pulled Nico up off the floor.

"You helped them set me up?" Nico said, his voice full of disbelief.

She stared at him with hate-filled eyes.

"I told you you were gonna get yours. And it gives me great pleasure to be the one to give it to you." She reached up and slapped Nico, hard. "I hope you rot in jail."

Joe laughed as he pulled Nico toward the door. "Let's go. Got to get you to your new home, ol' G."

As Joe led him away, I ran into Travis's arms. It was then that I remembered Sammy against the wall.

"Oh, no, Sammy." I raced to his side. He was bleeding from the stomach.

"Maya, I'm so sorry," he said, struggling to catch his breath. "I didn't mean to get you guys caught up in this. I'm so sorry." With that, he closed his eyes and I let out a scream.

Chapter 40

I stood over Sammy's wheelchair, slow tears trickling down my face. Yes, I was furious over all his lies, but how could I stay mad when he had literally taken a bullet trying to come to my aid?

"I'm gonna be all right," Sammy said, squeezing my hand.

I had been scared to death, but the bullet that had torn into Sammy had gone straight through him. It had been touch and go for the last three days, but he'd pulled through. I was still having a hard time processing that I was caught up in the middle of some drama like this. But you know your girl was working it. I'd done interviews with every news and entertainment outlet there was. (What? You didn't think I'd let an opportunity like this pass me up, did you? I mean, I didn't ask to be in the middle of this mess, but you'd better believe I'd worked it to my advantage.) Now, I was the media darling who had "survived a harrowing experience." (That had been the headline in *USA Today*.)

Of course, my mom, whom the police had told everything except for Travis's involvement, didn't want me to talk to anyone. But this was major PR and I wasn't about to pass it up.

"Are you ready to go?"

I looked over to the detective in the cheap, off-the rack suit. Two police officers in uniforms stood on either side of him.

"Can I just get a minute with my girl?"

"We're really not supposed to—" the detective said.

"Please?"

The detective looked at the two officers and nodded, and all three of them took a step back.

"Maya, I'm really sorry to have gotten you caught up in the middle of all of this, for getting Travis caught up. Don't be mad at your cousin. It really isn't his fault. He needed some money, and I presented him with an opportunity. The first time, he told me no. Then his mom needed that money for a transplant, and he felt like he didn't really have a choice. He really is a good guy."

"I thought you were a good guy," I found myself saying.

He shrugged. "Believe it or not, I am. I'm a good guy that made some bad choices. But I'm about to pay for those choices. To the tune of seven years to be exact." He tried to fake a laugh. "But Travis got a second chance, and I assure you, he's not going to mess it up."

I glanced out the window at my cousin, who was pacing back and forth in the lobby. The police hadn't told my parents about his involvement with the drugs because Sammy had covered and taken all the blame. I know he was scared to death about what would happen with him.

Luckily, Joe, the undercover cop, hadn't said anything. He'd given Travis a speech that had literally scared my cousin straight. I had a feeling Travis wouldn't so much as jaywalk after this.

I hated lying to my parents, for the simple fact that you had to keep up with lies and I had way too many important things to do to try to keep up with lies. But Sammy was right. Travis deserved a second chance, and I didn't want my parents sending him home.

It helped that Sammy had taken the blame for everything. When he'd come to, he'd told police that Travis had been there with him and he was the one responsible for everything. Nico and Margarita had tried to implicate Travis, but Sammy had stood by his story and so Travis wasn't charged.

"I just can't thank you enough for what you did for my cousin," I said.

He shrugged like it was no biggie. "Travis is good people. And he has a clean record. The last thing a young male needs is a record. This is my third strike. I'm going down regardless. No need to have Travis go with me."

I looked at him in awe. Most criminals would've had the "If I'm going down, you're going down, too" mentality.

"Can I ask you something?" I knew now wasn't the time, but since I'd found out my boyfriend was a drug dealer, several things had been seriously bothering me.

"You can ask me anything and I'll tell you the truth."

I looked at him like, *Seriously, I'm supposed to believe you'll be truthful now?* Even still, I said, "Do you remember I asked you about my classmate, Shay Turner, Jalen Turner's daughter? Did you get with her?"

He smiled. "I told you I didn't."

"You also told me you were a record producer. But that was just a big act."

"Ouch. Guess I deserved that one. I was just trying to impress you, that's all. But to answer your question, no. I never got with Shay. I met Shay a couple of times because I did business with her father."

"Did business? What kind of business?"

Sammy raised an eyebrow. "I was his weed guy before I graduated to the more powerful stuff."

I couldn't help but smile. So Shay knew my man was a drug dealer. That's why she had been smirking. Boy, this was definitely something I wouldn't live down.

"And the reason you didn't want me at your house? Do you live with your baby mama?"

"I hate that term. She's the mother of my child. We co-parent, but we're not together." He paused. "I kept stuff . . . in my place and just never wanted to put you in harm's way."

"And your crackhead uncle?"

"Just a dude I used to sell to."

"Why did you get involved in drugs?" I asked him, shaking my head as I processed everything.

"It's all I've known. Not making excuses, but it is what it is. Just make sure you tell Travis to leave this life alone. It ain't for him."

It definitely wasn't. I knew one thing, I was going to tell my dad about Aunt Bev's illness. Because it made no sense that Travis should have to resort to criminal activity.

"Maybe when I get out, I can take a page out your book. Find me something I'm good at and do it," Sammy said.

I nodded. I thought about his demos. He had the skills to make that happen. "Maybe you really can become a record producer. You have an ear for it."

She nodded. "Maybe I'll write me some songs while I'm doing my time."

"You can do it. You can do anything you set your mind to."

"Except get you," he said softly.

I smiled, but didn't answer because he was right. I liked him. I really did. But I didn't do drug dealers. Or liars. Or baby daddies. Or dudes facing seven years in prison.

"So, you gon' write to me in prison?" Sammy asked with a sly smile. My eyes widened and he laughed. "Yeah, a diva like you doesn't do prison."

I didn't know how to respond to that because he was right. As much as I cared for Sammy, my Louboutins wouldn't be clicking across any prison grounds, and I dang sure wasn't about to be some prison pen pal. So as far as I was concerned, this was good-bye.

Chapter 41

I took a deep breath, put my game face on, and dove in.

"What's up everybody, it's your girl, Maya Morgan coming at you for the latest episode of *Rumor Central*. Grab your shovels because I've got the scoop. You know the K2 craze that's sweeping the country? Well, we can tell you one area where they are clamping down on the disastrous drug. Right here in *Rumor Central*'s home base. That's right, if you're looking for K2 in Miami, you might have to look a little harder. That's because police have shut down one of the largest K2 rings in the country. They have the K2 kingpin behind bars and you won't believe who it is. *Rumor Central* has the exclusive details that brought down a drug network."

I pointed to the TV screen propped next to me showing video of a handsome man in an expensive suit being led into the police station. "Recognize this man?"

I waited for the nineties sitcom Donovan Davis used to star in to pop up on the screen. "Okay, what about now? You can catch him on reruns on Nick at Nite, but he hasn't done anything lately. That's because he hung up his Hollywood shoes and traded them for something a lot more lucrative. That's right, Donavan Davis was allegedly responsible for the pipeline that was funneling K2 into the States. He was apparently at the top of the food chain and after a two-year investigation, police have finally shut him down."

I turned to camera two and kept talking. "You know I once heard a very famous rapper say 'snitches get stiches,' but obviously the drug dealers of today don't live by that motto. Police struck a deal with notorious drug supplier Nico Caruthers, allegedly Donovan's top man. And in order to cut a deal, Nico sang like his name was Aretha Franklin. Yes, he told police everything he knows, and now it's our understanding that he's in a witness protection program. So, don't go looking for him. But if you want to find Donovan, his new address is the federal pen." I finished up that story, tossed to commercial, then came back and wrapped up the show.

I was actually glad when the closing music came up. Once I got the all clear I removed my earpiece.

"Great job, as usual," Tamara said, walking over to me. Dexter was by her side. They'd watched the show from the studio instead of the offices, where they normally watched.

"Yeah, it was good, but I still think you should've played up your part in everything," Dexter said.

"Nah, I'm good." I had gotten my fifteen minutes as it related to this whole drug thing. Now, I needed to go back to what I did best—regular celebrity gossip. This drug game was a little too real for me.

"I knew when I heard that message about you being sick, something was up," Tamara said as we walked back to my office.

"I wish you had followed your gut," I replied. "You're the one always telling me to follow my gut."

Tamara nodded. "You are right."

"Aren't I always?" I smiled.

"This could've ended very badly." Tamara shook her head like she was imagining everything that could have gone wrong. "I'm just glad it didn't. I can't go losing my star."

"Is that all you're worried about, losing your star?"

She laughed. "Or my mini-me."

I walked into my office and tossed my papers on my desk before doing a slow twirl. "No disrespect, Tamara, but I'm a tad bit more fabulous than you."

I loved our relationship because even though she was my boss, I knew she wouldn't take offense to that.

She smiled at me. "If that's what you gotta tell yourself, so be it. Enjoy your time off. You've earned it."

I told her and Dexter good-bye as I started gathering my things. Next week was spring break and our senior trip, and I was so ready to relax and have a good time.

On the drive home, I was thinking of all the fun I planned to have in Cancun, which was where we were going for our senior trip.

I got home to find Travis and Sheridan standing out front.

I pulled up and parked. "Hey, what's up?" I asked after I got out.

"Nothing," Sheridan said, glancing down.

Travis didn't say anything.

"What's really going on?" I held up my hands in defense. "And I'm just asking. I'm not trying to get in your business. I told you, I'm done. If you guys want to ride off into the sunset, then it's fine by me."

Sheridan stunned me when she said, "No, you were right. We shouldn't have hooked up."

I couldn't help but smile. "Oh, you're not really with that thug lovin', huh?" I joked.

Travis cut his eyes at me.

Sheridan shrugged and said, "Yeah, we can still be cool, Travis, but I'm not about that life."

He stared at her and simply said, "I understand."

Sheridan actually held her hand out for him to shake and this fool took it. I just laughed.

"That's all I wanted, Travis. Maya, sorry, I have to go. My mom is coming to town."

"All right. Talk to you later."

Both Travis and I watched her get into her silver Mercedes and drive off. I turned to my cousin, who was standing there just staring at her. Was he about to cry?

"I guess you're not used to getting dumped?" I said.

"Nah, I'm not. The bad part is I was really feelin' her. More than any girl I've ever been with. But she's right. She deserves better."

I draped my arm through his. "It's okay. You live and you learn." I leaned back and stared at him. "You have learned, right?"

He nodded. "Boy, have I ever." He turned to me. "I'm really sorry."

"I know you are."

We stood in silence for a few minutes, until he just abruptly turned and began walking inside.

"Travis, what are you doing?" I grabbed his arm to stop him.

He stopped, leaned in, and gave me a peck on the cheek. "I appreciate everything you've done for me. I really do. But I have to make this right."

I looked at him in confusion, but he just turned and walked back in the house. Of course, I quickly followed him. Inside the foyer, he made a left and went straight to my dad's office. He lightly tapped on the door.

"Uncle Myles, do you have a minute? I need to talk to you."

My dad looked up from his papers. I guess the seriousness of Travis's tone caught him off guard because he frowned as he set his pen down.

"Yes?"

Travis eased inside. I watched him from the hallway. I just knew he wasn't about to do what I thought he was about to do!

"I have something I need to tell you. I know you brought

me here for a second chance, a fresh start and I . . . I just . . . I just wanted . . ."

"Well spit it out, son," my dad said.

I immediately stepped up with a huge grin on my face. "He just wanted to say how happy he is to be here. He just finished telling me about how lucky he is to have a second chance." Travis stared at me while I talked. "So he just wanted to say thank you."

My dad smiled. "I'm happy to have you here. You're a part of this family, Travis. I actually was coming to talk to you in a little bit. I just got off the phone with Bev. I can't believe you all didn't tell me how sick she was."

"She told you?" he asked, shocked.

My father nodded. "Yes. But why didn't you tell me?"

"She wanted us to figure out a way ourselves," Travis replied. "I wanted to tell you so bad."

"That's what family is for," my dad said. "It makes no sense for her to be in need and not be able to come to me. It does no good for me to make all this money if I can't help out my own family." He leaned forward and sternly said, "Understand this, we are going to get your mother the best of treatment and she's going to be well taken care of."

It seemed like a tremendous weight was immediately lifted off Travis's shoulders. He relaxed and a slow smile crept up on his face. "I tried to tell mama that."

My dad smiled too. "Well, I think she knows it now."

"Well, that's just beautiful," I said, grabbing Travis's arm. "We're going to let you get back to work. Come on, Travis. Bye, Dad."

I pulled Travis out of the office. I didn't say anything until we were in his room, with the door closed.

"What were you doing?" I asked.

"I was about to come clean," he replied.

"Yeah. No."

"I was trying to do right." Travis sighed.

188 RESHONDA TATE BILLINGSLEY

"*Now,* you want to do right. You have a fresh start. Take it."

Travis looked around his room, then blew a long breath. "I guess you're right."

"I know I'm right."

He pulled me toward him in a bear hug. "Maya Morgan, I'm so happy to have you as my cousin."

I hugged him back, then stepped back. "As well you should be. It's not every teen that can survive being kidnapped and still come out more fabulous than ever."

"I love you, girl."

I smiled, and winked. "I love me, too. Holla!"

REAL AS IT GETS

ReShonda Tate Billingsley

ABOUT THIS GUIDE

The following questions are intended to
enhance your group's reading of
REAL AS IT GETS.

DISCUSSION QUESTIONS

1. From the start, Maya makes it clear that she doesn't cover stories this "real." Do you think she should've stuck to her usual gossip, or was it truly a situation where "her voice" was needed?

2. Maya is dead set against Travis and Sheridan getting together. Why do you think she was so against it? Whose side should she have taken when the two of them fell out?

3. Maya was always giving Sheridan a hard time, but she was in the dark about Sammy. Do you think she let things slide? What were some of the things that should've made her ask more questions?

4. Why do you think Sheridan was so blinded when it came to Travis?

5. Maya never wanted to get caught up in the drug scene. Why do you think she was so determined to "just say no"?

6. Sheridan told Maya, "You're supposed to be my girl. How could you not have told me about Angel?" However, when Maya first tried to tell her, Sheridan wouldn't listen. Should Maya have tried harder to come clean? Why or why not?

7. Should Tamara and Dexter have stopped Maya from going undercover? Do you think they had some responsibility as her employers to make sure she didn't do anything dangerous?

8. Margarita seemed to love her lifestyle with Nico. Why do you think she was the one who ultimately decided to turn him in?

9. Sammy took the blame for everything, letting Travis off free and clear. Why do you think he did that?

10. In the end, Travis almost came clean with his uncle, but Maya convinced him not to do it, saying everyone deserves a fresh start. Do you agree? Should Travis still have told his uncle about his involvement? Why or why not?

Rumor Central continues with
Truth or Dare

Coming in June 2014
Wherever books and eBooks are sold

Chapter 1

I couldn't stop smiling as I watched the commercial with white sandy beaches, crisp blue water, and hot-bodied people walking up and down the beach. In just a few days, that would be me. Of course, I would be a lot cuter than that busted-looking chick in this commercial. *Oh yeah, it was about to be on!*

"Stand by," my director, Manny, said, snapping me out of my daze.

I turned back to the camera to get my shine on (not that it ever left), but I got into serious focus mode when the camera turned on. As the popular host of the hottest celebrity gossip show—not just in Miami, but in the country—I always had to bring my A game.

"And we're back in five, four, three, two . . ." Manny pointed to me as the *Rumor Central* theme music came up.

"What's up, everybody?" I began. "It's your girl, Maya Morgan, and we hope you've enjoyed today's edition of *Rumor Central*. You'd better believe that we're all over this latest story about Usher, and you'll want to make sure you keep it locked here to get the latest scoop. But you'll have to tune in two weeks from now because your girl is out! That's right,

I'm heading to Cancún, Mexico, for a little fun in the sun, rest, and relaxation, and an all-around great time at the world famous Spring Break Fling!"

This weeklong event had been going on for a few years, but in the past couple of years, celebs started going and that took things to a whole other level. Granted, I was going with my senior class, but I wasn't about to tell my viewers that. I didn't need the world to see I was getting excited about a high school thing. But make no mistake, I was excited.

Manny gave me the cue to wrap, so I said, "Yours truly will be all up in the mix, so enjoy the break. I know I will. Until next time, holla at your girl."

The theme music came up again as the credits started rolling. I couldn't get my earpiece out of my ear fast enough.

"Bye, Manny," I called out, not bothering to wait for a reply. I was so ready for a vacation. Since I'd started as host of *Rumor Central,* I had become a workaholic, which wouldn't be so bad if I wasn't seventeen and in the prime of my teen years. But hey, you couldn't be on top—and stay on top like me—by being a slacker. As Diddy says, "I'll sleep when I die." So, I wasn't making plans to sleep in Cancún, but I *was* going to kick it. Even though my girl Kennedi didn't go to school with us in Miami (she lived in Orlando), I'd managed to finagle her on to this trip. (Hey, when you were a rich chick like me, you made your own rules).

Anyway, between Kennedi and my other BFF, Sheridan, this was going to be nothing but fun.

"Looks like somebody is ready to go," my executive producer, Tamara, said, approaching me as I speed-walked down the hall back to my office.

"Well, that's the understatement of the year. I am so ready to get out of here," I replied, stopping to face her.

Dexter, the show producer, stood next to her smiling mischievously. Dexter was Tamara's partner in crime and ever since they had canceled the reality show, *Miami Divas*, which

I starred in with four other people, and given me my own show, they were always conspiring with one another.

"Uh oh," I said, my gaze darting back and forth between the two of them. Whenever Dexter got that look in his eyes, something was up. It meant his mind was churning.

I glanced at my watch. I had fifteen minutes before I was off. So I didn't need his mind to be churning with anything concerning me.

I decided I wasn't even going to ask question. "Umm, okay then, I'll see you guys in two weeks," I said, trying to step around them.

"Hold on," Tamara said, following me. "We're going to walk with you to your office."

I looked back and forth between the two of them. "I'm off in fifteen minutes."

"This will only take ten," Dexter said, giddy like he was hiding some big secret.

"Okay, what's up?" I said. I walked in my office and started gathering my things. I would listen, but I didn't want to stop and make them think I was giving them too much of my time.

"Well," Tamara said as she exchanged glances with Dexter. "We know you're about to head to Cancún with your friends and Dexter and I were talking . . . "

Dexter was so excited that he couldn't even let her finish. "And we think now would be the perfect time to take the show on the road."

"Excuse me?" I said, finally stopping and giving them my undivided attention.

"Think about it," he said. "Maya Morgan in Cancún with young celebrities from all over the country? Oh, that's some good juicy material waiting to happen," Dexter said.

I couldn't believe they were going there—again. When I'd first started the show, it was bad enough that I had to turn my back on my *Miami Divas* co-stars. My BFF, Sheridan, had since gotten over it. But the others—Shay Turner, Bali Fernandez, and Evian Javid—were still salty about it. So, I felt bad about that (for a brief minute anyway), but then I'd had to sell out my friends for ratings and that had created major drama. Now here they were, asking me to do it again.

Tamara must've been able to tell where my thoughts were headed because she said, "You talked about wanting to go international. This is the perfect opportunity."

"This is supposed to be my vacation!" I protested.

"Sweetie, do you think Beyoncé takes a vacation?" Dexter said.

"Ummm, as a matter of fact she does," I replied.

"No, trust and believe, I assure you she's still working even while she's on vacation," Dexter said.

"We're not trying to take away from your fun. We're just saying now would be a perfect time to have a camera crew go on the road," Tamara interjected.

I shook my head. I was so not feeling this idea. "I just want to relax and have a good time."

"And you can," Tamara said. "If we send a camera crew, we're footing the bill."

I looked at them sarcastically like *that* was supposed to be enticing to me. I could foot my own bill. As a matter of fact, this trip had already been paid for.

"Everything's already taken care of," I said.

"So, you have the penthouse suite at The Intercontinental Presidente?" Tamara asked matter-of-factly.

"How do you know where we're staying?"

"Honey, we know everything," Dexter said, folding his arms and flashing a sly smile.

"Well, no, I don't have the penthouse suite. We tried to get it, but they told us it was unavailable."

Both Tamara and Dexter smiled. "It's unavailable for normal people. Not for a network like WSVV," Tamara said.

"So picture yourself in the penthouse," Dexter added. "I

mean, you're already the 'It' chick and I'm sure you have a very nice room, but we've booked the whole top floor of The Intercontinental Presidente. The penthouse suite just for Maya Morgan."

That made me raise an eyebrow.

"We'll make sure you have a driver, unlimited food and drink—non-alcoholic of course—everything at your disposal. We know you can do all of this yourself, but why bother? Let us do it for you," Tamara said.

I narrowed my eyes. "And all I have to do is agree to let you film the trip?"

"That's it," Dexter said with a smile. "Let us film it and *Rumor Central* gets the scoop."

"And we'll even give you your free time," Tamara added. "Just get us enough for a few stories and the rest of the time is yours."

I wasn't feeling this idea because I really was looking forward to just relaxing, but images of the penthouse suite, a driver at my disposal, and an all-around good time on someone else's dime, made me say, "Fine, I'm in."